Caroline Fothergill

Diana Wentworth

Vol. I

Caroline Fothergill

Diana Wentworth
Vol. I

ISBN/EAN: 9783337066031

Printed in Europe, USA, Canada, Australia, Japan

Cover: Foto ©Andreas Hilbeck / pixelio.de

More available books at **www.hansebooks.com**

SELECTED LIST.

A DREAMER OF DREAMS. A Modern Romance. By the Author of 'Thoth.' Crown 8vo, 6s.

" Unmistakably delightful.......The wit and philosophy and poetry of the book are no less striking than the grace and charm of the author's style."—*St James's Gazette.*

"Original and artistic.......Comes very near to being a tremendous feat of fancy."—*Athenæum.*

HOW I SPENT MY TWENTIETH YEAR. Being a Short Record of a Tour Round the World, 1886-87. By The MARCHIONESS OF STAFFORD. With Illustrations. Crown 8vo. [*Immediately.*

Second Edition.

GOSSIPS WITH GIRLS AND MAIDENS. Betrothed and Free. By LADY BELLAIRS. New Edition. Crown 8vo, 5s.

"An admirable manual of self-help and self-education ; an encyclopædia of valuable hints and suggestions. Even matters that might be called familiar, trivial, or commonplace are brightly treated with fresh originality. Directions are given as to diet as well as study ; stress is laid on the due development of the physical powers and the careful preservation of health ; dress and the adornment of the person are not neglected ; maidens are counselled as to the choice of a husband, and as to how they may cage as well as net an eligible admirer."—*Times.*

Third Edition.

BODY AND SOUL. A Romance in Transcendental Pathology. By FREDERICK NOEL PATON. Crown 8vo, 1s.

WITH STANLEY'S REAR-GUARD—MAJOR BARTTE-LOT'S CAMP ON THE ARUHWIMI. An Account of River-Life on the Congo. By J. R. WERNER, Engineer, late in the Service of the État Independant du Congo. With Map and numerous Illustrations.

FOURTH EDITION.

SARACINESCA. By F. MARION CRAWFORD, Author of 'Mr Isaacs,' 'Dr Claudius,' 'Zoroaster,' &c. Fourth Edition. Crown 8vo, 6s.

"'Saracinesca' is a very remarkable book, and a great advance upon any of the author's previous works."—*Academy*.

"It is a book of which even the greatest masters of fiction might with reason have been proud."—*Pictorial World*.

"Clever, striking, interesting."—*Spectator*.

"The book is something more than a clever novel; it is a literary success."—*Vanity Fair*.

A NEW AND CHEAPER EDITION.

LIFE OF PRINCIPAL TULLOCH, D.D. By Mrs OLIPHANT, Author of 'The Life of Edward Irving,' &c., &c. With a Mezzotint Portrait, and Wood Engraving of the Study at St Mary's College. Third Edition, post 8vo, 7s. 6d.

"Mrs Oliphant has drawn the Principal's portrait with a loving hand, but its fidelity will be acknowledged by all who knew him well. It is as lifelike as the striking head on the frontispiece of the volume."—*Times*.

"It would not be easy for 'fellows' without a heart and mind of unusual proportions to talk as does this great Scotchman throughout this delightful book."—*Daily News*.

"This is an ideal biography.......In this delightful volume there is nothing 'set down in malice,' and scarcely anything that one does not read with interest and pleasure."—*St James's Gazette*.

"Mrs Oliphant has performed a labour of love in giving to the numerous admirers of Principal Tulloch this vivid and faithful portrait of her old friend."—*Pall Mall Gazette*.

"Principal Tulloch has been fortunate in his biographer.......We have nothing but praise for this pleasant memorial of a lovable and kindly man."—*Athenæum*.

WILLIAM BLACKWOOD & SONS, EDINBURGH AND LONDON.

DIANA WENTWORTH

DIANA WENTWORTH

BY

CAROLINE FOTHERGILL

AUTHOR OF 'AN ENTHUSIAST,' 'A VOICE IN THE WILDERNESS'

IN THREE VOLUMES

VOL. I.

WILLIAM BLACKWOOD AND SONS
EDINBURGH AND LONDON
MDCCCLXXXIX

CONTENTS OF THE FIRST VOLUME.

CHAP.		PAGE
	PROLOGUE,	1
I.	PROFESSOR WENTWORTH'S WILL,	10
II.	MOTHER AND DAUGHTER,	13
III.	A FRIEND,	26
IV.	A LOVER,	41
V.	THE END OF A JOURNEY,	74
VI.	JACEWO,	99
VII.	THE CURTAIN RISES,	113
VIII.	NEAR THE FOREST,	141
IX.	BY THE LAKE,	158
X.	"CARISSIMA,"	182
XI.	GLAMOUR,	210
XII.	IN THE FOREST,	227
XIII.	IN DOUBT,	247

DIANA WENTWORTH.

PROLOGUE.

IT was an exquisite summer evening, not moonlight, but not yet dark, so that the young man and woman walking slowly along the West Fields could still dimly see one another's features. They were very young: he looked about twenty, she could not be more than seventeen. He had a tall well-made figure, and a face which expressed resolution and a certain degree of pride, although his clothing was that of a country work-man, and his speech bewrayed him as a dweller among the hills. The girl was very pretty, with soft brown hair, and eyes which were alternately appealing and roguish. One sought in vain in her features for some sign of the high purpose which animated his, yet, in spite of this want, it was a very winning face. She wore neither bonnet nor shawl, so that it was easy to see that her figure was slighter and more upright than is the case with most girls of her class, and the arrangement of her dress be-spoke an evident knowledge and ap-preciation of her advantages. She had slipped her hand through the young man's arm, and rather nestled against him as they walked along. The light was fading fast; the river rushing at the foot of the cliffs, on the top of which they were walking, made its presence known to the ear rather than the eye; the outlines of the hills, which rose around them on all sides, were becoming dim; the woods on the other side of the valley were an indistinct mass. They had walked for a long time before they began to speak. Then the man said—

"It's a bonny spot, Mary lass; I shall often think of it when I am far away."

"Eh, John," she answered, with a little toss of her head, "you are a queer fellow. Any one else would have told me they would think of me."

"I shall think of you. This place and you are so bound up in my mind, I can't think of one without the other. We have walked here so often together."

"An' now I mun walk alone. It'll be dree work. Are you boun' to go to-morrow, John?"

"Yes; I'm off in the morning as soon as it's light. I shall walk to Bellingham, and take the train from there."

"And you can't tell when you'll be back?"

"Nay, how can I tell? I've my fortune to make; but as soon as I can come back, I will."

"I doubt it will be a long time to wait," she said, with a sigh.

"And what if it is?" he answered

rather quickly. "You won't be waiting alone; I shall be keeping you company, though I am a long way off. You don't think you'll get tired of waiting, Mary?" he concluded, rather anxiously.

"No," she answered, "no; I won't get tired, though it is a dull place, and there is very little to see. But I shall be glad when you've made your fortune; then you'll be a rich man, and I shall be a lady."

"It's not only riches as makes ladies and gentlemen," he said; "it's many a lot of other things besides; and I doubt if ladies and gentlemen is any happier than us poor folk. They've just as hard a time in many ways, and I can't tell why you hanker after it so. A good, honest, working woman's better than an idle fine lady; and if you were a lady, Mary, you would be an idle one, I fear: you're not fond of work," he concluded, half playfully.

"No," said Mary, "I'm not. It's a life as would suit me finely, to ride i' my carriage and do nothing all day, because there was servants to do the work. Eh, I should like to have servants, and to keep my hands white and clean."

He laughed at her tone of enthusiasm, and then said more gravely—

"I can promise you servants, if you will only have a bit of patience. And now, Mary, we must say good-bye. Here we are at your father's farm, and they will be angry with me if I keep you out any longer. Promise me once more to be true."

"Eh," she cried, "how you do go on! Do you doubt me?"

"No, I don't doubt you; but I don't like leaving you so long. You are very pretty, and there will be lots of men asking you to wife. And maybe they will try to persuade you at home; they have not much faith in me, you know."

"John," she cried, with a sudden tone of fear in her voice, "you never can tell. If father began wishing me for to marry some one else, and you not here to help me, I'd happen say Yes for peace and quietness. Let me swear, and then I shall be quite safe; I *could* not break an oath."

"I don't like oaths," said John; "I would rather have an honest promise from some one I trusted."

"Ay, but John, to please me," she pleaded. "We will swear to one another, and then we shall both be safe. Do now, John; it's the last thing I shall ask you for a long while."

"Well," he said, slowly; "but it's to please you, mind."

"Yes, yes; and you swear first."

So he swore. "I, John Garthwaite, swear to be true to you, Mary Metcalfe, as you are true to me."

And Mary said the oath after him.

"I, Mary Metcalfe, swear to be true to you, John Garthwaite, as you are true to me."

Then there came the last parting, kisses, blessings, and a few last words, and then Mary went into her father's house, and John set off home across the hills.

CHAPTER I.

PROFESSOR WENTWORTH'S WILL.

PROFESSOR WENTWORTH was dead and buried, and his will had created a certain sensation among those who heard it, and those who heard of it. It was an un-English will, and those who talked about it said that if he had not all his life been an eccentric man, there would have been grounds for thinking him of unsound mind when he died. To his sons, aged respectively twenty-three and eighteen, he left five hundred pounds apiece — all his savings. He had money invested, which was bringing in a hundred and fifty pounds a-year, and this he bequeathed to his widow and only daughter, to be shared equally between them until his widow's death, when it should all go to his daughter. There was a letter directed to his sons, which he had desired they might read after hearing his will, and in which the following passage, relating to the way in which he had left his money, occurred :—

"I have done my best for you, and now you are both started in life, and must look to yourselves alone. With five hundred pounds to fall back upon, you cannot come to harm. It is in accordance with what I have taught you all your lives, that the women must have the settled income. Your sister may never marry, in which case she must be provided for; or, if she does, she cannot go penniless to her husband."

The lads were fond and proud of their sister, and had acquiesced in their father's judgment. Wilfrid, the elder, was well placed in New Zealand — Harold, the younger, was in a large Whitfield warehouse; clearly it was Diana, beautiful fastidious Diana, who must be provided for, and shielded from the wintry winds of care and privation. As for their mother, they were both good sons, and would always care for her. They thought their father had acted quite rightly, and went back to their work perfectly contented with what had fallen to their share.

CHAPTER II.

MOTHER AND DAUGHTER.

"It is from your uncle Philip, Diana; you may read it," said Mrs Wentworth, handing her daughter an open letter.

Diana put down her mother's breakfast-tray, and sat down on the edge of the bed to read the following letter :—

"My dear Alice,—I have your letter telling me of your changed arrangements. I think it is a pity Harold cannot make up his mind to stay in England near his mother; but since Wilfrid is doing so well in New Zealand, I suppose it is only natural that he should wish to share his good fortune. Young blood will be young blood, and life in a Whitfield warehouse cannot be as attractive as sheep-farming in New Zealand. I wish the lad every success. Under the circumstances, I think it quite natural you should wish to leave Whitfield, and I feel gratified that you should ask my advice as to a suitable place for your future home. I need not assure you that, were it necessary, any help could give you in the expense of re- moving I would willingly offer. I have, however, another proposal to make, which trust will prove agreeable to you. You cannot live in comfort anywhere upon

the income to which you have been re-
duced, and I write now to suggest that
you and Diana should henceforth make
your home with us. I have consulted
Guy and the girls, and I need scarcely
say that they join with me in offering
you a hearty welcome. Your income will
be sufficient for your personal wants; and
as your presence in my house can only be
a help and an advantage to my girls, I
think the arrangement will be a mutual
gain. Of Diana I cannot speak, since I
have not the pleasure of knowing her;
but I trust she will be happy with her
cousins. Perhaps I am biassed, but I
think intercourse with Gertrude and
Dora cannot fail to influence her for
good."

There was much more—plans, arrangements, and sympathy; but all breathed a
confident spirit, as though the writer felt
sure of his invitation being accepted, and
the letter concluded very affectionately
with a hope of a speedy meeting.

Diana having finished reading, let her
hands sink into her lap, and sat looking at
her mother.

"How like your uncle!" said Mrs Wentworth, enthusiastically. "What a noble,
generous offer! and what a simple way
out of all my difficulties!"

"What does it mean?" asked Diana;
"I don't understand it. Have you been
writing to uncle Meredith about money
matters?"

"I wrote to tell him that as Harold is

going to join Wilfrid in New Zealand,
there is no further need for us to remain
in Whitfield. I asked his advice about
a cheaper place to live in, and just hinted
that I should be very thankful for any
help in the expense of removing, or even
for permanent help if he could afford it.
This constant anxiety about money matters will drive me into my grave before
long. I would not say a word against
your poor father; but I really think he
might have contrived to leave me a
little better off. However, now it is
all at an end, thanks to your uncle. I
thought he would send me a cheque;
but I never anticipated such generosity
as this."

Diana said nothing, and her mother went

on, having only paused for an instant to wipe her eyes.

"Dear Philip! it is just like him; and the thought of passing the rest of my life in the old Abbey, the happy, happy home of my girlhood, is almost too much for me. What an unspeakable relief it will be to have everything one wants again, and not to be constantly counting the cost of every little thing! I shall feel quite young again. I shall write at once and tell him how grateful I am for his kindness. You, of course, will do the same."

"Nay, mamma," said Diana; "I have nothing to write about. I did not ask for charity. I do not need it, and I am not going to accept it. I have no gratitude to express."

"I beg you will not talk in that foolish way," said Mrs Wentworth, with some show of irritation. "When I accept, my acceptance will be for us both; your home must be with me."

"I shall not go to Garshill," said Diana, in a voice which was neither loud nor excited, but which expressed unshakable determination.

"It is quite useless to talk in that way. I shall not allow such behaviour to my brother."

"I don't know him: I have never seen him, or any of my cousins. I know nothing about him, and he knows nothing about me, or I don't think he would ask me to go and live at his house," with a sudden gleam of something very like

wickedness lighting up her face. "Just
listen how he speaks of me! he seems to
think I am a child yet," and she picked
up the letter again, and read aloud the
few words relating to herself. Then she
threw the letter aside and laughed, standing in the middle of the room with a
satirical smile curling her lip.

Mrs Wentworth looked at her without
speaking, and with a peculiar look in her
eyes. What she saw ought to have filled
her heart with a glow of joy and pride,
and instead she looked gloomy and dis-
satisfied.

She saw before her a tall slim girl of two-
and-twenty, with a face and figure of mar-
vellous beauty. Hair and eyes were dark,
the eyes very large and clear, the com-

plexion very fair and delicate. Her
features had been moulded in an expression of command, and the general
habit of the face was rather proud than
sweet. Her whole face and bearing were
full of spirit and resoluteness, yet her
figure was delicate to fragility. There
was something about her which would
have made even a stranger feel instinctively that she had her whole life before
her, and that it would be very difficult,
in spite of her two-and-twenty years, to
forecast the use she would make of it.

It has been said that it was a sight to
fill a mother's heart with pride, and that
Mrs Wentworth looked only gloomy;
perhaps the slight air of defiance in the
rounded upturned chin irritated her, for

her voice was not altogether sweet as she said—

"It is a long time since I saw your cousins; but Gertrude was then very handsome, and Dora an exquisite fairy-like creature. Their father is quite right in thinking them charming, and I quite agree with him that intercourse with them would do you a world of good."

Diana laughed again; laughter was very often on her lips.

"I have no doubt they have every imaginable beauty and attraction," she said; "but I have not the slightest desire to make their acquaintance, nor have I any intention of doing so."

"You make me very angry," said her mother.

"I will go now," said the girl, taking up the breakfast-tray. "I suppose you will get up. We can talk about this later."

She went down-stairs into the sitting-room, and stood looking out of the window. It was a dismal winter morning, fog, melting snow, and rain filled the street. She stood for some time lost in thought, and then with a quick graceful movement turned to the inside of the room, saying half aloud—

"I'll write now, while I am alone. I would rather starve than go to live there."

She got writing materials and began her letter. Judging from the smile which so often lit up her face as she wrote, she had reason to be satisfied with her work; but

there was that in her smile which made
one feel doubtful whether her uncle would
be equally pleased.   When she had finished, she folded and addressed her letter,
saying—

"Now, my sweet cousins, I wonder if,
after this, you will be so anxious to have
me, and yet it is polished and perfectly res-
pectful, in fact 'deadly polite';" opening
her letter again to once more run her eye
over its contents.   "That is one of the
greatest benefits of civilisation; it enables
you to sting people beyond endurance,
without casting a shadow on decency and
politeness."

She leaned her elbows on the table, and
catching sight of her own reflection in an
old-fashioned round mirror which hung

against the opposite wall, she smiled frankly at herself.

"One is handsome," she murmured, "and the other is an exquisite fairy-like creature. I am not afraid of them." There was a pause, during which she continued to gaze into her own eyes, reflected in the old mirror. Then she spoke again, "She did not say they were clever," and she smiled once more.

CHAPTER III.

A FRIEND.

At that moment the maid-of-all-work knocked at the door and said, "Dr Sherlock."

Diana rose from her seat in surprise.

"Tom!" she cried; "what are you doing at large at this time of day?"

"I am not busy this morning, and it is so long since I saw you, I thought I would just look in in passing. How is your mother?"

"Very well, and I am very glad to see

you. There is something to relate, and I want you to hear it from me first."

She told him about her uncle's letter, and the proposal it contained, her expressive face all alight with varying emotions as she sat looking up at the tall young man standing on the hearth-rug, his eyes fixed upon her face, as if he did not want to look at anything else.

He listened in silence : it was a way he had, and sometimes Diana liked it, and sometimes it roused her impatience. This time she liked it. Her mother might come down at any moment, and she wanted to tell her story first.

Tom was still silent when she had finished. He was slow in everything, slowest of all in speech. He was a tall plain young man, with nothing remarkable about him except a very beautiful complexion and an odd drifting way of walking, which made every one smile. He was a young doctor, working his way steadily upwards, with no relatives or connections to help him on, accustomed to look to himself alone, and quite satisfied with his solitary position in the world. He had known the Wentworths for some years before he had come to settle in Whitfield. Diana and he had been fast friends ever since she was a child, and now the hope of some day winning her for his wife was the only feeling which equalled in strength his wish to get on in his profession.

He remained silent for so long that at last she looked up at him again, and said—

" Well, are you too surprised to speak ? "

" I don't know. What are you going to do ? "

Each word dropped slowly and separately from his lips, and when he spoke, one heard that his voice was very flexible.

" Mamma is in raptures ; she is going to accept."

" Oh ! Do you think you will like it ? "

" I am not going."

" You won't go ? "

" I think I would rather starve. Ever since I read the letter, one of my favourite mottoes has been running in my head : ' It is better to dwell in a forest, haunted by lions and tigers, the trees our habitation, flowers, fruits, and water for food,

the grass for a bed, and the bark of the
trees for garments, than to live among
relations after the loss of wealth.' That
is a pagan proverb, and I like it."

"Good for the pagans," said Tom, slowly.
"That is very vigorous; but it wouldn't do
in our climate, you know."

"No," said Diana; "as a medical man,
of course, you could not countenance it.
But I can do what comes to the same
thing, — put up with anything rather
than go."

"But what shall you do?"

"I have not quite made up my mind
yet; but I think I shall get a situation of
some kind."

"Oh!" Dr Sherlock pulled his moustache thoughtfully, and then ventured on

the mild remonstrance, "Do you think your father would have liked it?"

"I don't think he would have objected," said Diana, with a little hesitation.

"Well, but I do," replied Tom.

"You see," said Diana, and the fact that she condescended to an explanation impressed Tom very much, — "you see, I shall not be really working for my living. I have plenty to fall back upon, and I shan't trouble about a large salary. But if I do definite work in exchange for my maintenance, I shall be independent. I will not receive benefits, I should be so hampered afterwards. I should never be able to do anything to which uncle objected, because of past favours. I could never endure it,—I must be free. I might

as well go to prison at once, as live in that
way. I should be chained hand and foot
with invisible chains."

" What kind of man is your uncle ? "

" I have never seen him."

" Then he may be a monster for anything we know."

" He thinks I am a monster, and I will
tell you why. Years ago, six or seven,
before he had the accident which made
him the invalid he has been ever since,
he came over here to see mamma. We
were sent for, of course, and the boys
went, bribed by promises of gold watches
and chains, which, to be quite fair, were
honourably given to them. I remember
I had been in disgrace all day, and was
very angry with mamma, so I refused to

go. Repeated messages were sent; but I
paid no heed to them, and when I heard
that uncle was coming to the schoolroom
to see me, since I would not go to see him,
I ran out of the house and stayed away
until I was sure he was gone. He was
deeply offended, of course. Can't you imagine the rage of the rich man, accustomed
to have every one bow down before him,
when he was spurned by a poor relation?"
She leaned back in her chair, and laughed
delightedly at this recollection of the past.
"And I never feel sorry I did it: I have
no doubt it was a wholesome check to his
pride. He never forgave me, and I was
never invited to the Abbey. The boys
have been often, and always came home
laden with gifts, amongst which there was

never anything for me, to my great joy.
But you see he has borne malice all these
years, and would have gone on all his life,
if this had not happened. I would not
live in his house for the world. I should
feel suffocated in it."

Dr Sherlock's face had grown very tender as he sat and listened to her. He
realised, not for the first time, how tem-
pestuous and impulsive this girl's nature
was; how passionately she felt about even
little things; and with how dogged a determination she would do battle for what
she believed to be right, — and her right
was seldom that of the world at large. He
understood that she looked upon her isola-
tion and estrangement from her mother's
people as in some way conferring dis-

tinction upon her, even though it had orig-
inated in a mere fit of girlish naughtiness.
She was very full of faults, and she did
not make the most of such virtues as she
had; yet Tom loved her dearly, and the
thought of such a girl going out to work
seemed pitiful to him. An older man
might have said it would bring her just
the discipline she needed; but Tom did
not think of that. Nevertheless he felt
instinctively that this was not the right
moment for making the only alternative
proposal which seemed to him good. Instead he said—

"No, you must not go: it is not the
right place for you; you would not be
happy there. We must see what else can
be done. I will come in again some

evening, and we will talk things over
at our leisure. Perhaps your friend Mrs
Burland might be able to suggest something."

"I will see. Must you go? Come in
again as soon as you have time."

"One thing first, Diana," he said,
hesitatingly. "Don't speak so bitterly of your mother: it is not fair, you
know."

"It is true," said Diana, knitting her
brows. "You know, Tom, that mamma
and I do not get on; and that is another
reason why I will not go to Garshill.
Mamma and I have lived together long
enough. It is her own doing; she herself got me out of the way of living with
her."

"I wish you would try to forget that, or to look at it in a different light. Your mother thought she was acting for the best."

The girl's face hardened as she said—

"She did it because she wanted to be rid of me. She condemned me to four years of *misery*, when there was no need for it, and I shall never forgive her."

"Well, good-bye, Di. Remember me to your mother, and tell her I will look in again soon."

When he was gone, Diana stood by the fireplace, with all the light gone out of her face. He should not have called up those recollections just then, because when her father died she had made a resolution that she would try to live on better terms with her mother. A year had gone by since then, and she had kept her resolution fairly well, but she was not happy at home; and now that both her brothers had left England, and a change was inevitable, she was determined that the change should be to her own advantage.

Mrs Wentworth was, in the opinion of most people, a very charming woman. A few, Tom Sherlock amongst them, thought differently, but that was the general verdict. Unfortunately she had never known how to live in harmony with her daughter. Diana had always been difficult—from her earliest childhood a strange mixture of apparently diametrically opposed qualities and characteristics — a very ill-balanced mind, many people said, and Mrs Went-

worth fully agreed with them. When
Diana was fourteen, her mother decided
that she had utterly outgrown home in-
fluences, and that she must go to school
at once—to a school, moreover, where the
strictest discipline should be rigorously
enforced. Such a school was difficult to
meet with; but the right place had event-
ually been found, and for four years Diana
had led a life of pure misery in it. She
came home for her holidays, each time feeling more embittered against her mother,
and the last two years had been spent
entirely at school. She knew that her
mother had sent her from home because
she had no sympathy with her, and she
judged her with the pitiless intolerance of
youth. This four years' banishment from

home-life had in some degree moulded her character, and was partly answerable for the cynical view she took of domestic happiness, family affection, and other accepted facts of life.

CHAPTER IV.

A LOVER.

DIANA got her way: Mrs Wentworth yielded, after a not very strong show of resistance. Secretly she was of her daughter's opinion, that they had lived together quite long enough; and she was well aware that life in the old home, with her brother and two affectionate attentive nieces, would be much more comfortable without this daughter, between whom and herself there seemed always a tacit coldness and misunderstanding. She knew her brother would

not approve of Diana going out as a governess, so she said very little about it.

Diana had no great difficulty in meeting
with a situation, for her father's will rendered her independent of salary, although
she said that on principle she should take
what was offered to her. She had been
anxious to go on to the Continent, and
the situation she finally decided to take
was in Polish Prussia. Her employers
were called Camphausen, and they lived
at a place called Jacewo, a place of which
no one had ever heard, which considerably
increased Diana's wish to go there. There
was a large family—three sons and three
daughters, the eldest girls aged respectively seventeen and sixteen. Diana was
to be companion-governess to them, and

to share the family life. She at once made up her mind to go there, and her mother only ventured the remonstrance that it seemed a very long way off—three days' journey, without stopping even a night on the way. Diana bore down all opposition, and without consulting any one, wrote to Frau Camphausen to settle the matter, and arrange the time and manner of her journey.

She and her future employer had exchanged letters by return of post, so that the whole business had been settled in about a fortnight. During that time Dr Sherlock had been very busy, and had had no time to see the Wentworths, so that he had heard nothing of Diana's plans. He came in on the evening of the day

on which she had written to accept the
post, and she lost no time in telling him
all about it. They were alone, for Mrs
Wentworth was busy packing and arrang-
ing for her removal to Garshill.

"I am so glad it is settled," she said,
when she had finished. "I was afraid some
obstacle might arise at the last moment."

The animation in her face found no reflection in her companion's features.

"It is a long way," he said, slowly.

"That is why I like it. I want to get
as far from here as I can—thousands of
miles away."

"What for?" asked the doctor, bluntly.

"I am weary of this place. I never
want to see it again."

"Oh!" was all his reply; but she heard

him murmuring in his deliberate way:
" Bad for me that."

She said nothing, and presently he went
on—

" I don't like the whole thing; there is
something unnatural in it. You were
never made to work for your living;
and I am very much opposed to your
going."

" I am not going to work for my living:
it would be rather a dismal prospect if I
were, for they offer only a very small
salary."

" Suppose you fall ill."

" Suppose the world comes to an end."

" I don't know how your mother can
consent to your going."

Diana smiled as she answered—

" She is glad."

" I wish you would not speak in that way," said Tom, looking distressed. " I do not like to hear it."

" What is the use of trying to disguise the truth? you might as well try to clothe a deformed man so that he should look straight. Mamma and I feel crookedly towards one another, and always shall. We cannot live together any longer."

" What has happened? Have you quarrelled?"

" What need is there to quarrel? It is the constant dropping that wears away a stone, not pouring a bucketful of water over it."

He made no answer; he had scarcely heard her. He was thinking that the

time to speak had come, and he felt
horribly shy, and very anxious and
doubtful as to the result. She said no
more, and he began to feel his way
cautiously by saying—

"I do wish you would give this up,
Diana."

"I can't, Tom. I wrote to Frau Camphausen to say I will go as soon as she
wants me."

"That doesn't matter. Write again, and
say that on consideration you don't want
to go so far from home, and she must find
somebody else."

"I am counting the days till I go," was
her only answer.

"What do you know about these people?
They may be very disagreeable."

"I have no doubt they are ogres at the very least."

"You are running a great risk."

"I run a risk every time I skate or dance or drive. In fact," fixing her beautiful eyes upon his face, "I must go; if I gave it up I should have to go and live at Garshill, and I *will not* do that."

"No," he said; "that is not the only other thing to do."

His heart beat very fast, and he felt that now he must go on. But he got little encouragement from the rather puzzled look which came over her face.

"I can't see any other," she said, at last.

"I'll show it to you, then. I don't want

you to go and live at Garshill; there is no need. I want you to come and live with me."

He was looking hard at her as he spoke; indeed there was an almost stony expression in his eyes, so nervous and uncertain did he feel. For a moment she returned his gaze—wide open and uncomprehending; then a light seemed to break in upon her, and she began—

"Do you mean——?"

"I mean that I want you to be my wife; yes, that is what I mean."

He heaved a great sigh of relief as he realised that he had at last said what had been on his heart, and he waited anxiously for her answer.

"Tom!" she said, in a tone of utter

incredulity, which brought the colour into his face.

"What do you mean?" he asked. "Why do you speak like that?"

"O Tom, how could you ever think of such a thing!"

"Do you mean to say that you have never thought of it?" he asked, completely losing his head.

"Thought of you as a husband? never— not once. As my comrade and my best friend, who has often taken my side when every one was against me,—I have always thought of you like that, but never as anything else."

"I have never thought of anything but that; and won't you begin to think of it too? Do, Diana."

" Oh no ; it is quite impossible."

"Why ? " he asked, desperately. " I
don't see it."

" I can't," she answered. " I simply
can't."

" I have loved you so long and
so truly. I can't believe there is no
hope."

"You would not like me to say ' Yes '
when I do not love you."

" No, I wouldn't — yes, I would. I
would rather have you in that way than
not at all."

"O Tom, don't talk so foolishly ! I
can't imagine what put such an idea into
your head ; you must have seen I never
thought of such a thing."

" Oh, I know you are not to blame," he

said bitterly; "but still I thought you liked me."

"I do—that is, I did; but if you go on talking like this, I shan't like you any more."

Her eyes flashed, her foot tapped the floor. Her temper was quick, and her patience soon exhausted; neither did Dr Sherlock show to advantage as a disappointed lover. He had nothing to say to this outburst; and after a pause she went on—

"If I married you, I should be chained here for the rest of my life. I should live and die here. I know nothing but Whitfield, and I should never know anything else."

"It is your home," he said, rather stolidly. "I don't know what you mean by talking in that way."

"Of course it is my home : that is the very reason. Do you never get tired of home ?"

"Never. I love it; I become more and more of a home-man every day. If you would only marry me, it would be perfect."

She laughed a little unsteadily before she answered—

"You see how utterly unsuited we are to one another. We should always be acting in opposition to one another."

"I don't think it follows at all. People who marry should not be too much alike."

"Still less, too much unlike," she answered quickly, and then they were both

silent. Diana was sitting in a low chair
in front of the fire, and after her own last
words, she leaned back and clasped her
hands at the back of her head, so that
her arm hid her face from Tom. She
wished that he would go. Her nerves
were naturally highly strung, and just
lately she had been going through a good
deal. Tom's attitude and manner jarred
upon her, and made the temptation to
speak sharply almost irresistible. As the
minutes went on and he said nothing, she
began to find the silence almost more than
she could bear, and she bit her lip, in her
endeavour not to show her nervous irritation. She was absolutely heart-whole ; no
man had as yet touched her feelings below
the surface, and she was powerless to enter

into Tom's state of mind. She only felt angry with him for having spoken at all. When she did at last speak, her words were not calculated to comfort him.

"I am so tired of Whitfield: that is why I want to go to this particular place, Jacewo. However disagreeable it and the people may be, they will at least be fresh and different from what I know here. If only for that reason, they are to be preferred."

"That sounds as if you were fickle."

"I daresay I am fickle. I get tired of things and people. I don't think I could keep to the same affection for ever and ever."

She was saying the first thing that came into her head, out of pure contrariness, and

her mood was not improved by Tom saying with great solemnity—

"You are talking like a child : it is very
wrong to talk like that."

"It would be the height of folly to
marry now," she went on, ignoring his
interruption.   "I have seen nothing of
life, and know very few people. I want
to see life, and it would be ridiculous to
tie my hands at the very beginning; afterwards I might easily meet some one I
liked better than you, which would be
very awkward."

It was natural to her to express herself
with a little exaggeration; but her words
were not devoid of wisdom, except to
Tom, who did not like them at all, and
said—

"I should think you have seen as many men as other girls, with your father and brothers, and the open house you have always kept."

"Do you think I call those people I meet at dances and picnics and tennis men? You are the nearest to a man I know here, but I can conceive that even you might be surpassed."

"You are very unkind; and just let me tell you what I have been thinking. You say you are tired of your home, and this place, and everything about you. I believe that is only because you have never been without them. I don't like this idea of your going away in the least; but we might do this. I won't ask you to marry me now. After all, though I could offer you a home, it is not such as I should like you to have, and I should not have spoken so soon, if it had not been for this scheme of yours. Go to this outlandish place, since you have set your mind upon it: it may teach you to appreciate what you despise now. In the meantime, I will work hard for us both. I am making two hundred a-year clear now; will you promise to come home and marry me when I am making four hundred?"

"Am I to be banished out there till then? Condemn me to transportation for life at once, and have done with it."

Her scoff brought the hot colour into his cheeks, and he answered warmly—

"You are unfair and insulting, Diana. Do you suppose I have not got it in me

to make a decent livelihood by my profession ? "

" I hope you may make a hundred thousand a-year, as long as you don't ask me
to share it with you. I don't *want* to
marry you, Tom. I wish you would take
my answer, and leave me."

" I won't. You ought to marry, Diana.
You have got a lot of queer crotchets,
which only make you unhappy. If you
got married, you would soon forget them
in other things."

There was truth in what he said, but
there was also truth in Diana's answer.

" You are not the man to make me forget crotchets, Tom."

There was a note of sadness in her voice.
Beautiful and brilliant though she was, she

had too marked an individuality ever to be popular. She had many acquaintances; but the portion of love which had fallen to her share was small. She and her mother were hopelessly at odds, and perhaps each was equally to blame. Tom was the first man who had asked her to share his life, and although she rejected his offer, she felt that he would probably be the last. She was touched by his faithfulness, and she inwardly marvelled when he repeated—

" Will you promise what I ask?"

She did not speak. Some time before she had risen from her chair, and now she stood with one foot on the fender, her elbows on the mantelpiece, her face shaded by her hands. Some inspiration held Tom

from disturbing her meditations. He had
no idea what was passing in her heart, nor
how empty it felt, nor how the emptiness
ached in a dull gnawing way, as the
empty socket aches after the tooth has
been taken from it. At last she turned
round. Her face was pale, her eyes
burned beneath the contracted brows. She
looked at him for a moment. Her lips
were so firmly closed, it seemed as if she
had difficulty in opening them to speak.
At last she said—

"I cannot engage myself to you; but
if you like, I will promise——"

"Yes—what?" he interrupted, eagerly.

"Not to engage myself to any one else
until we meet again."

He had expected more, and his face fell.

"Why do you offer this?" he asked at last.

He did not understand her in the least; he felt puzzled and uneasy at her manner.

"To give you satisfaction. You have been very kind to me, and we are old friends; you deserve something."

"But I don't see that I am getting anything," he said, speaking more from embarrassment than boldness.

"Oh yes," with equal gravity, "you are. As long as we do not meet—for this promise dates from my leaving Whitfield —you will have the satisfaction of thinking, when you do think of me, that I am free, and if not engaged to you, at least not engaged to any other man. And so," with a smile beginning to hover round

her lips, "if you are wise, we shall never
meet again."

Bitter disappointment kept him silent
for a minute. She had succeeded in rousing
his slow but lasting anger.

"Is that your way of dismissing me?"
he asked at length. "It is ingenious and
womanlike, truly."

"Softly, softly; will you have my
promise?"

He looked at her, and his anger blazed
up anew. He had learnt his lesson at
last, and he saw there was no hope for
him. He felt just then as if he never
did wish to see her again, and if she
would not be his, he could at least pre-
vent her marrying any one else. That
was something: his blood boiled up, and

speaking quickly, almost savagely, as if he feared she might change her mind, he said—

"Yes; I will have it. Promise me that after you leave Whitfield you will engage yourself to no man till we have met again. Get a Bible, and swear it to me."

"Nay, I will not swear. You often call me a pagan, and with a pagan her word is her bond. I promise on my honour that, after leaving Whitfield, I will engage myself to no man until you and I have met again."

"I am satisfied," he said, solemnly; and she, having recovered her spirits, laughed at his gravity. There was no weak place in her heart, and she gave the promise with the greatest assurance.

Directly after this he went away, and

as he went out at the house‑door, he met a young lady coming in, with whom he exchanged salutations. She said—

"I suppose Diana is at home;" and on his saying she was, the girl went forward unannounced, and knocked at the drawing-room door.

Diana greeted her visitor with some surprise.

"You, Amy!" she said; "what has brought you out at this time of night?"

"I have not seen you for a week, and I wanted so much to hear if you have come to any arrangement with those German people."

She sat down as she spoke. She was a fair girl of middle height, with undecided manner and speech, and yet with some-

thing in her face which seemed to denote
obstinacy. She formed a strange contrast
to Diana, yet she was the only girl in all
Whitfield who stood on terms of anything like intimacy with her. The
deeper feeling was on the side of Amy
Fairbairn, who often served as a vent to
Diana's overwrought feelings. It was unfortunate that she had come just now;
Diana had not yet recovered from her
interview with Dr Sherlock, and she was
not in the gentlest mood. She told Amy
that she was going to Jaccwo, and Amy
said—

"How dull it will be when you are gone!
But perhaps you will not like the place,
and will be back again soon."

" If my esteemed friend Tom Sherlock

could have had his way, I should stay
here for ever. He has just asked me to
marry him."

"O Diana, I am so glad! I hope you
accepted. Did you accept? It would be
so delightful if we lived in the same town:
we might be married on the same day.
If you had to wait, I should not mind
waiting too."

"Take care how you make rash promises.
Tom explained his position to me very
clearly, and had I accepted him we might
have looked forward to a possibility of
marriage in the next world, it would certainly never have taken place in this.
If you and your Cartwright decided to
wait for me, you would have every prospect of dying an old maid."

Mr Cartwright was the curate, to whom Amy was engaged; waiting for preferment as a necessary preliminary to marriage.

"You say such strange things, Diana. Is Dr Sherlock so poor?"

"Very poor; but he had the generosity to offer me a share of his poverty."

"Then you refused him?" said Amy, blankly.

"Yes; although he made another generous proposal. He wanted me to wait for him out at Jacewo; no doubt he thinks it is a safe place, where I shall not meet with the temptation of a more brilliant offer."

"I am sorry," said Amy. "His practice is here, and so is Reggie's curacy. We might have lived here together all our lives."

"How is your Reggie?" asked Diana. "Is he any better?"

"Yes, he is better; but there is still infection, and I may not go near him. It is very hard I can do nothing for him. When mamma is poorly, I brush and comb her hair gently, it soothes her so; but I cannot even do that for him."

"Of course not. He might think you wished to assume the mastery, if you began to comb his hair. It would be most unwise, and might cause your engagement to be broken off."

She spoke with a gravity which made Amy feel uncertain as to her meaning. Strong as was her affection for Diana, she was often at a loss to know whether she was in jest or earnest.

"I heard of such a sad thing yesterday," she said presently. "Mr White of the Carlton Road Bank has died suddenly, in the prime of life, leaving a widow and a large family."

"I wonder why it is," said Diana, "that men with wives and large families so often die in the prime of life. Poor men, I mean, only poor men have those large families. I suspect they do it in self-defence. They see they have got into a hopeless muddle, with only one way out of it comfortably to themselves, and they naturally take that way, and leave the others to get on as they can."

"I don't think such a way would be natural at all; it would be very selfish."

"It would be natural because it is selfish."

She spoke almost gloomily. She was leaning forward with her chin in her hand, her dark eyes looking into the glowing coals, her mouth set in a cynical curve.

"I am very sorry for Mrs White," said Amy, "she is such a weak, delicate woman. If you think like that, it will be useless for me to ask you what I was going to."

"Do you mean to join in a subscription?"

"Yes; I am trying to get a little sum together."

"I can't help you. It would only encourage others to do the same. If I ever found a charity, it shall not be for destitute clergymen or poor widows' children, but for old maids who have fought

their way through life against great odds,
and have at last come to the end of their
resources."

Amy said nothing. She was one of
those people who remain comparatively
indifferent to the privations and sorrows
of older people, but who "cannot bear to
see the little children suffer." Besides,
she took no interest in old maids. Who
does? She thought Diana hard and cold,
and rose from her seat, saying—

"I shall go home. I can't talk to you
any more. You are not nice to-night."

"I will not keep you if you would
rather go. Good night. I will let you
know when I leave home."

When she was alone again she resumed
her seat by the fire, looking gloomily

into it; but her thoughts, whatever they might be, were not uttered aloud.

Amy walked home in a glow of indignation against Diana and of satisfaction with herself. Yet every now and then the thought of her friend's deep sad eyes and gloomy speech penetrated to her heart and made her feel uncomfortable, and as she walked along she murmured—

"Poor Diana! I wish she were happier, and I believe she would have been if she had accepted Dr Sherlock."

CHAPTER V.

THE END OF A JOURNEY.

NEW Year's Eve was the date fixed for Diana to arrive at Jacewo, and a fortnight before that day she left Whitfield and went to her friend Mrs Burland, in London: a day or two later, Mrs Wentworth went to Garshill. Diana could not have spent her last days in England with any more congenial companion than Antoinette Burland; she entered fully into the difficulty of the girl's position, and sympathised entirely with her refusal to

go to Garshill. She could sway Diana
when no one else had the slightest influence over her, and Diana trusted her
implicitly. Antoinette had opposed to
the utmost Mrs Wentworth's decision to
send her daughter to school, and although
her counsel had been disregarded, Diana
had never forgotten that the effort had
been made. The oases in that four years'
desert of existence had been Antoinette's
visits, letters, and hampers. Now she
discussed her plans with a sympathy and
insight which soothed Diana's wounded
spirit, and which not even Amy had
shown. They had parted friends, and
Amy's last words had been to urge
Diana to bear in mind her promise, that
when she returned to England, her first

visit must be paid to the future Mrs
Cartwright. Mrs Burland's only misgiv-
ing was regarding the long journey, more
than half - way across Europe, and she
was anxious that Diana should let Mr
Burland see her safely to her destination.
She scouted the idea, and would so evidently have been angry if the plan had
been persisted in, that Antoinette let it
drop.

.   .   .   .   .   .

She had made her last change in trains;
in less than an hour she would be at
Jacewo. She was alone in the railway
carriage, and she let down the window
and leaned out. She had passed through
many patches of wood at an earlier stage
of her journey; now she seemed to be

travelling through an endless forest. The tall pine-trees rose straight and motionless, almost within reach of her hand. She crossed the carriage and leaned from the opposite window, the same sight met her eyes. The train was running on a single line, which went straight on into the forest. She looked back, the trees had closed in upon the narrow road, the line traced by the finger of civilisation. She looked forward, and at no great distance the railroad appeared to melt into the trees; the train seemed imprisoned in the heart of the forest. A chill feeling of loneliness crept over her, and for the first time she began to ask herself where she was going, and what would be the end of this long journey. Jacewo! Where was Jacewo? She did not know. How was she to know when she had reached Jacewo, and what kind of a place would it be? She could not tell; she knew nothing of it all. She was going she knew not whither. A feeling came over her that she was going where strange things would befall her; as though she had turned a corner in the road of life, and unproved sights and experiences lay before her; as though she had entered a new world, and a voice which she did not know, yet could not disobey, was calling her to advance in the darkness.

The moon rose higher, and she could see more plainly. From time to time there came a clearing amongst the trees, and, stretching away in the distance, she saw glittering white expanses, frozen tracts of water which occur here and there in the forest, now silvered by the light of the rising moon. She looked at them in fascination, with this strange feeling of awe growing stronger and stronger in her heart, until at last the trees grew thinner, the train slackened speed, and at last stopped. She saw a kind of shanty, and a platform of rough earth frozen hard as iron, and then she hastily looked at her watch: it was already some minutes past the time when the train was due at Jacewo, and she again put her head out of the window and asked of a man who was running past if this station was Jacewo. He answered "Yes," without pausing or turning his head, and she collected her things and got out of the train.

Her luggage placed safely on the ground, and the train having steamed slowly out of sight round an immense curve, which made it look like an enormous serpent, she turned to a group of men who stood near, looking at her with a good deal of curiosity, and, according to her instructions, asked if the Camphausens' carriage was at the station. One of the men shook his head, and when, at his request, she repeated the name, he said he knew it not, he had never heard it before. The other men drew near, and took part in the conversation. A few questions, asked in Diana's quick, rather imperious way, and in German which, though perfect in grammar and structure, betrayed her nationality in accent and tone, brought out the fact that this station was not Jacewo, but only a kind of small goods station, little more than a signal-box; that the train she had left was the last; and that there was no village anywhere near, where she could get either shelter or a conveyance to take her to the end of her journey.

She did not hesitate to reproach the men with their perfidy in letting her leave the train and giving her her luggage. The culprit shrugged his shoulders, and turning to his companions, a sort of council was held, in which the deliberations were carried on in Polish. Diana, being left to herself, also set her wits to

work, although she had told the men
that as they had got her into this difficulty, she left it to them to find her
a way out. It had just occurred to her
that she might be able to telegraph to
the Camphausens and ask them to send
the carriage on to her, and she was just
going to make the suggestion when one
of the men turned to her and said he
thought it possible that she might be
able to finish her journey at once. It
appeared that a gentleman had driven
over from Jacewo in the afternoon, it was
not known if he had gone back. If he
had not, they knew where to find him,
and they were sure he would be glad to
share his carriage with her; should one
of them go and see after him?

"Certainly," she said; and when the messenger had departed, the other men invited her to go into the signal-box until he returned. She was accommodated with a chair by the stove, and sat looking out of the window into the forest. The moon had now risen fully, and the night was almost as light as day, with a cold clear light in which the pine-trees looked like ghosts, and the perfect stillness of the place was almost oppressive. She began to believe in the actual existence of bears and wolves, not as likely visitants on this particular night, but as living creatures with an existence outside books. Her companions talked together in Polish, and from time to time addressed her in German. The messenger had already been

absent some time, and they spoke openly
of the small chance of the gentleman from
Jacewo being still in the neighbourhood.
Fearless by nature, Diana felt no terror at
her position : it never occurred to her that
these men could have sinister intentions
towards her, and she was perfectly ready
to intrust herself to the care of the unknown man, whoever he might be, if he
were still at hand and willing to be bur-
dened with her. She only felt annoy-
ance at being stopped so near the end of
her long journey, for she was tired; and
also, after having insisted on travelling
alone, it was a little humiliating to find
herself in this difficulty, and she quickly
made up her mind never to mention it to
her friends in England.

She was warm and comfortable, and as she sat looking out on the mysterious forest, wondering how the Burlands were spending this New Year's Eve, and how they imagined her to be spending it, the door opened, and the messenger came in, and communicated with his fellows in his own tongue. Then he turned to her and told her he had had a long search for "den Herrn Ingenieur," as he called him, but he had at length found him, and he was perfectly willing to accommodate her in his carriage, which was even now at the door. If she would take her seat in it, he would join her in a moment; he was still in the forest.

She lost no time; she was out of doors almost before he had finished speaking, and the men followed her and began to pack in her luggage. The carriage was a truly aboriginal vehicle, like an immense basket on wheels, filled with straw, and with a plank placed across it for a seat. In front, on a plank to himself, sat the driver, an aged Pole, in sheepskin coat and cap and green woollen gloves. He appeared to have the utmost confidence in his own power of guiding the four small restive horses which were harnessed to this primitive chariot.

Diana stood looking on at the group of men, who, with many exclamations, and what seemed the exercise of superhuman strength, were getting her boxes into the cart. She was smiling at them in some derision, when, out of the shadow of the trees, a man emerged into the moonlight.

He saw her before she saw him, and he stood still for a minute to look at the English girl standing there alone, the spirited bearing of her slight figure noticeable even in the muffling of the long garment, trimmed and lined with fur, which she wore. (It was a parting gift from Mrs Burland, and Diana had caught it closely round her, to protect her against the stinging cold.) This man was accustomed to see and judge at a moment's notice, or even less; and his keen eyes ran rapidly over the girl's face and figure, as she stood there unconscious of his presence. He noted everything, the beautiful proud features, the slight touch of haughtiness in the face, caused by the cutting of her nostrils and lips, the exquisite setting

of the head, the resolution and courage
expressed in her attitude. Her face was
half turned towards him, and he could
see both her smile and the brilliance and
depth of her eyes. It was a beautiful
sight, and as he looked at her, he mut-
tered—

"Is it possible?   There must be some
mistake."

What he saw stirred him; there remained yet to hear her voice, and he was
on the point of stepping forward to accost
her, when the men, having accomplished
their task, fell back, and he saw her take
out her purse.

"That, too, is an indication of character," he thought, and waited a moment.

She took out a piece of twenty marks, he saw the gleam of gold in her hand, and gave it to one of the men, saying in German, which surprised him by its purity—

"Divide it amongst you, and drink to me : it is New Year's Eve ; wish that I may have everything I want in the new year."

"We will wish you a handsome husband, Fräulein," said the man, touching his cap.

"A husband ? Ah no," with a little laugh,—"that I could have ; wish me everything I *want*."

The listener raised his eyebrows and smiled as he heard her. She must be very young. In spite of the dignity of her bearing and her chiselled features, youth was in every line of her face and figure.

She had just been delivered from a very awkward position, and the chances were a thousand to one that she would never set eyes on any of these men again. The little scene showed that heart and hand were equally open.

But he had seen enough. He came up to her and raised his hat, saying—

"You are the lady who got out here by mistake?"

"You are English!" she said, turning to him in her quick way.

"Why, yes; did they not tell you? I was told at once that you were a com- patriot."

"They did not say what you were; they spoke of you exclusively as the 'engineer.'"

"I am an engineer, and an English one."

"I am so glad. I took it for granted you would be German, and I feared you would smoke,—I do so dislike tobacco."

He bit his lip to hide a smile. He liked to hear her speak; her voice was clear and delicate, suggestive of lifelong intercourse with people of culture.

"It is so kind of you to give me a seat in your carriage," she went on. "I am exceedingly grateful to you."

"I beg you will not mention it; I am only glad it is in my power to do you any little service. And now, my men," he went on, for they were again occupied with her boxes, "make haste, or the lady will be frozen."

He turned to help Diana into the carriage, saying—

" You had better take your seat at once :
it is fearfully cold, and you must be tired.
Are you properly wrapped up? What is
this made of ? " touching her long mantle.

" It is lined with fur," she answered,
just turning up a corner of it that he
might see.

" Sit at this side," he said, as she was
moving to the other end of the plank,
having got into the vehicle with perfect
ease and disregard of his offer of help.
" We shall drive fast, and the wind comes
like a knife across the plain. If you keep
at this side, I shall somewhat shelter you
from it."

They were off, flying along the highroad at the reckless rate at which Polish
horses generally go, and Diana, feeling

very wide awake and intensely alive to everything around her, sat upright on her hard jolting seat, and let her eyes wander over the wide monotonous plain over which they were driving. Everything was distinctly visible in that clear moonlight, and distant objects looked strangely near. She shivered as she looked. It was so silent, so lonely, so unlike anything she had ever seen before. She glanced at her companion; she had not yet seen his face clearly, and she could not see it now. His fur cap was pulled down on to his head, and the fur collar of his overcoat was turned up to his ears. He was tall, and she liked his voice and manner, with a touch of authority in it which seemed natural to him. He sat in silence, his chin sunk in the fur on his coat, his hands buried deep in his pockets. He appeared quite unconscious of her presence, which was a new experience to her, and caused her to smile.

While she was looking at him, he suddenly raised his head, and his keen grey eyes met hers. He looked straight at her for a moment, and then said—

"Well, and where am I to set you down when we get to Jacewo? I did not hear where you are going to."

"I am going to some people called Camphausen;" and as he said nothing, she went on, "do you know them?"

"Yes, I know them. They told me they were expecting an English lady to live with them; but I had forgotten, and it would never have entered my head that you were the lady."

"Why not? Do I not look like one?"

"Heaven forbid! But there are ladies and ladies: they have different manners, and one associates a certain manner with a certain calling. If I may say so, you do not look in the least like a governess."

"I am not one yet; I do not begin till to-morrow."

"And you have never been one before?"

"I will not try to conceal that this is my first attempt."

"Do you know anything of these people?" he asked, after a pause.

"Nothing at all. Since you do, will you tell me something about them?"

"I know nothing to tell. They are not

interesting; they are very respectable, and
think very highly of themselves."

" Respectable people always do; they
mould their opinions on their reputation."

"Are you really going to be the
children's governess?"

" I am really. Perhaps you do not
think I look competent, and I must
frankly confess that I have no certifi-
cates."

" I do not think you are accustomed
to failure," was his somewhat ambiguous
reply, and then his chin sank back into
his coat-collar, and he said no more.
Neither did Diana speak again; the only
human sound came from the old driver,
who urged on his horses ever faster and
faster, till they seemed to fly over the

ground. Presently "the engineer" roused himself, and pointed to where at some distance before them a group of lights was visible near the ground.

"Those are the lights of the Jacewo railway station," he said; "we shall soon be at your destination now."

Ere long they reached the railway, and drove across the line; the barriers—tall, tapering white poles — were lifted, and showed sharply against the clear sky. Immediately afterwards they crossed another line, then the ground rose a little, and in another moment they stopped.

The house-door was opened almost before they had left the carriage, and a bewildering scene of arrival and explanation followed. Diana was aware that she was shaking hands with her countryman, and thanking him for what he had done for her, then the door closed after him with a bang, and he was gone.

CHAPTER VI.

JACEWO.

By the time Diana had been a month at Jacewo, only pride prevented her from shaking the dust of the God-forgotten spot from her feet, and turning her steps elsewhere. Every one who knew her had opposed her coming out here, and she had persisted in it; she was resolved, therefore, to bear a great deal before confessing that they had been right, and that she could hold out no longer.

She did not get on with the Camphausens. Frau Camphausen had never been pleasant, and she could not resist telling Diana that she had all along been opposed to her coming, from the moment she had seen her photograph. She had only reluctantly yielded to her husband's representations that Miss Wentworth's name would be such excellent practice for the children. The children themselves found no more favour in her eyes: she was not naturally fond of children, and this particular family possessed characteristics and qualities which roused her deepest dislike and repulsion. The four younger children attended the local day-schools, the two eldest, Minna and Hedwig, studied with her, and she spoke English to, and superintended the preparation of

the lessons of all. All the children inherited their mother's handsome features;
but they were ill brought up, ill-mannered,
and selfish. They had been governed
from babyhood by force, and understood
no other authority. The two elder girls,
being of an age to appreciate personal
advantages, were jealous of her. Her life
was very monotonous, and the social
pleasures hinted at in Frau Camphausen's
letters consisted almost entirely of sitting
in the drawing-room in the evening and
plying her needle. Frau Camphausen was
a magnificent animal, attached to her
children solely by her physical relation-
ship to them, ambitious that they should
do well at school, and make a good show
in the world, because if they failed, the

discredit of their failure would be reflected upon herself. In their home
training, morals and mind had been left
to take care of themselves, and all the
energy had been concentrated in bringing
their physical points to perfection — as,
for instance, they always wore strong
walking-boots in the house, lest their feet
should deteriorate in shape; and Diana's
slender and daintily slippered feet were
regarded by the girls with envy, and by
their mother with disapproval. Their
dresses were ugly and unsuited to their
age; but they were pretty enough to
triumph over that, and had not thought
much about it, until Diana came with her
well-made gowns and indescribable air of
wearing them. All her ways and works

were opposed to theirs, and it was no
wonder she did not fall into her place in
the family. But Frau Camphausen bore
with her. Her music and singing were
good, and her English and French irre-
proachable; and she had accepted without
a murmur a salary which was small even
for a private governess in Germany.

Jacewo was an ugly little town, with
narrow squalid streets, and no public
buildings of any size except the prison,
from which prisoners now and then es-
caped, and fled over the frontier into
Russia. There was a shabby town-hall,
a shabbier synagogue (half the population
were Polish Jews), and a Lutheran church,
which surpassed even the other buildings
in shabbiness. There was also a ruined

Polish church, standing a little way out
of the town, with the remains of a square
tower, upon which storks built their nests;
and a burial - ground, which was strewn
with bones and skulls which had been
thrown up when, a grave being full, the
latest occupant was evicted, to make room
for a new-comer.   There was a cemetery,
but that, too, was overcrowded, and a new
one had been made; but, as Diana ob-
served in the sarcastic letter which she
wrote to Mrs Burland, descriptive of her
new surroundings, it seemed as yet designed more for the use of the living than
the dead, for while no one had been buried
in it, it contained five garden-seats, and
was used as a kind of public promenade.
The town stood in the vast plain of East-

ern Europe, in surroundings dreary beyond description. In that wonderfully
clear atmosphere one could see for many
miles. Diana, standing at the schoolroom
window, could see the train coming in
from Pawlowsk half an hour before it
reached Jacewo. The only variety, and
that was repeated until it became monotonous, was the vast stretches of dark
pine - wood. Lines of pine - trees fringed
the horizon, and patches of the same
formed the only shadows in all that
shadeless land. There was something
impressive in the very flatness and monotony of the landscape—on so large a
scale it was rescued from the commonplace. Diana, although by nature a lover
of the hills, did not escape the influence

and fascination of this "fringe of Siberia";
the character of the country got into her
mind and coloured her thoughts.

In spite of being uncomfortable, and
aware that she was not regarded with
favour by her employers, she was not
unhappy. She was eager and speculative
by nature, and the difference in family
life, with the relics of Polish manners and
customs which came under her notice, interested her; and she was too indifferent
to the people among whom for the present her lot was cast, to be disturbed by
their want of affection for herself. She
lived curiously apart from them, and was
affected merely objectively by what she
saw. She felt no disgust or concern of
any kind when she saw Herr Nowakow-

sky, seated opposite to her, take a boiled
egg from its cup, divide it lengthwise
by a cunning stroke of his broad-bladed
table-knife, scoop out half the egg, and
tip it down his throat from the end of
the same knife. She only looked at him
with curiosity and interest, and wondered
how he did it, and whether he had had
to practise very long before he succeeded
in accomplishing the feat without any
personal risk. She did not lose her self-
control or equanimity when she saw Frau
Camphausen kick her eldest son, a lad of
thirteen, in a rage, or thump her eldest
daughter's shoulders with her fist, when
in the same frame of mind. She only
raised her eyebrows, lifted her lip in a
half smile, and generally left the room

with her head a little higher than usual.
She listened with absorbed interest when
she heard the youngest boy (a child of
eight, and the most inveterate little liar
that ever breathed) invent a long and
complicated string of falsehoods in answering his mother's questions as to why
he had been late in coming home from
school. She never complained of the
children to their mother, she never offered
any remark on their manners and customs; but her face was very expressive,
and take it all in all, she was amply
revenged for Frau Camphausen's often
studied rudeness and neglect, by the
embarrassment which appeared in that
portly lady's face when, in the midst of
some lecture, chastisement, or catechism,

she encountered Miss Wentworth's calmly critical eyes and composed countenance, with its half-amused, half-cynical expression. Diana herself never punished the children; she taught them what she had undertaken to teach, but declined to interfere in any other department.

Her compatriot she had not seen again, but she had heard of him from time to time, and the information she got may be condensed into the following :—

He was an engineer employed by the German Government to construct a new line of railway between Jacewo and Berg, a town on the Russian frontier. His name was John Garthwaite, and he came from England, but from which part of England no one seemed to know. He divided his

time between Jacewo and Berg, and when
at Jacewo lived at the Adler, the principal
hotel in the place. He could visit at any
of the houses in the town; but availed himself of his privileges to only a very limited
extent, being by nature (so Diana was
told) reserved and self-contained, to a degree unusual even among Englishmen. He
was shut out from a good deal of social
pleasure because he did not play cards,
and cards were the chief amusement of
the people of Jacewo. Women played as
vigorously as men, and Frau Camphausen's bosom friend, Frau Olawska, would
sit down to the whist-table in the evening, and remain there all night until eleven
o'clock the next morning; but then she
had no family, as Frau Camphausen al-

ways said in defence of her friend. As
Diana merely received the information
which was volunteered to her without
asking any questions, she got no idea of
Mr Garthwaite's character. It appeared
that, the very day after her arrival at
Jacewo, he had gone to Berg, and had
been there ever since, nor was he expected to return for some time yet.

As the weeks went by, she began to
wish Mr Garthwaite would come back.
She was tired of the Camphausens, and
he would be some one fresh, and then she
had never really seen him; she would not
know him again were she to see him, except from the fact that he would probably
look like an Englishman. She thought
that the situation was rather amusing,

and she also enjoyed the reflection that
nobody else knew there was any situation,
for in her letters to England she had mentioned neither the mistake she had made,
nor the existence of such a person as John
Garthwaite. Now, she felt herself in the
position of the King of Bavaria, sole spectator of a most interesting drama, arranged
for her enjoyment alone, and upon which
the curtain might go up at any moment.

CHAPTER VII.

THE CURTAIN RISES.

It had been with great unwillingness that John Garthwaite had gone to Berg, the morning after his meeting with Diana. He very much disliked the whole Camphausen family. He had heard all about their project of having an English governess; they had taken him into their confidence, and had discussed the subject in his presence frequently, with constant appeals to his judgment and opinion. In the midst of it he had gone to Berg for some time, and when he came back the matter had been settled, and he heard with complete indifference that a suitable English lady had been met with and engaged. Later, he was told with some excitement that she was to arrive on New Year's Eve; but he had straightway forgotten all about it. As far as "Miss Ventvort" occupied his mind at all, she figured as a middle-aged woman, worn with toil, and hardened by a long struggle to keep her place in the world; with few ideas, and those narrowed by limited experience and monotony of existence—in fact, the typical "governess," as she existed years ago. The governess had come; by an accident he had made her acquaintance before she had met her employers

and their family. He had seen her, and
talked to her, and he would never forget
her; he felt that at once. After leaving
the Camphausens' house, he had gone to
his hotel, and had sat for hours smoking
and lost in thought. He wondered how
Diana would find herself in the new life
and surroundings. He had had no experience of governesses, and while ad-
mitting his ignorance, he could not persuade himself that the young lady whose
acquaintance he had just made was a fair
representative of the class. She had none
of the attributes of a woman accustomed
to earn her own living. The very *douceur*
she had given the men at the station
showed either culpable recklessness or
the comfortable knowledge that there was

plenty more money where that came from.
He knew very little about women's dress;
but he had an idea that the garment in
which Diana had been wrapped was a
costly affair, and that the fur with which
it was lined, as she had so obligingly
turned up a corner of the mantle that
he might see, was very superior to anything he had so far seen worn by the
ladies of Jacewo. He wondered who and
what she was; he thought of her all evening; he could not get her out of his head.
He wondered what she was doing at that
moment. Had she had supper? Was
she answering the questions which would
be poured upon her? Had she gone to
bed early, tired with her long journey?
Was she sad, disappointed, home-sick?

Or was she curious, alive, and interested? Most probably the latter, he thought; and he hoped it was so.

He could not help thinking of her: he had known very few women, and none like Miss Wentworth. She was a new type and a revelation to him. He was the second son of a Yorkshire dalesman; his parents had been middle-aged when he was born, and by the time he was of an age to take notice of people's appearance, his mother was merely a hard-featured woman, old beyond her years, and without beauty of any kind to arrest the eye. There was his cousin Susan, who was like his sister, but she had lived at his home since she was a child, and was fast becoming what his mother was.

It is true he had once loved, and his love
had been a bonny lass; but that was over
now, and she had been in no way like
this girl he had just seen. He had led
too busy a life to think about women.
His father had been an unsuccessful man,
poor, and as proud as unsuccessful people
are apt to be. He had shunned intercourse with his neighbours, and had
bidden his boys do the like. The elder
son was at home,—he had inherited the
bit of land at his father's death. John
had been early apprenticed to the engineer from whom he had learnt his profession. He had worked hard, for it had
been made clear to him betimes that he
would have no one to look to but himself; and as his calling had been his own

choice, persisted in against the will of his parents, he had been expected to justify that choice by rising high in his profession. There was every external inducement, added to natural love, to work hard, and for years he had given little thought to anything outside his work. Now he had his reward. Though still young—thirty-three — he had risen high. His name was known beyond the limits of his own country; his opinion had an influence out of all proportion to his years; and he was consulted and deferred to on matters of great public weight in his profession. He had made a good deal of money already, and there was every prospect of his becoming a rich man among rich men. At present he chiefly valued his money

for a reason which was known to no one
but himself. It was thirteen years since
he had been home; but he knew the immense disadvantages under which his
brother laboured, and he foresaw that,
sooner or later, he would come to the
end of things, and would be obliged to
sell the old farmstead. Few people ever
heard John Garthwaite speak of his birth-
place; but none the less had he a deep
and abiding love for it, and it was his intention to become the purchaser whenever
his brother should want to sell it. Up to
the present time, he had had no other
thought in amassing money. He knew
the time to which he looked forward would
come, and it was his intention to be
ready for it. Thus, almost his whole life

had been spent in work, with rare and
short intervals of leisure, leaving little time
for intercourse with women; and to tell
truth, he had not hitherto regarded this
deprivation in the light of a hardship.
That bygone experience had left a bad
taste in his mouth, and he rather shunned
than sought them, nor had the ladies of
Jacewo been destined to correct his taste.
Hence the fact that, in speaking to women,
he forgot to lay aside the manner he wore
in talking to men. The air of authority,
and abruptness of speech, which had
pleased the one, Diana, offended the ninety-
and-nine of Jacewo and elsewhere, and
had earned for him the reputation of being
rough and disagreeable. He forgot to
make allowances for their weakness, or,

in deference to custom, to outwardly yield
the point which he inwardly maintained.
He contradicted them, judged them on
their merits, and exposed their short-
comings in a way which was rendered even
more exasperating by the way in which
it was done, which showed a perfect un-
consciousness of having offended. A fine
lady, with languid airs, and indifference
to everything which was worth knowing
and doing, was an abomination to him;
and there had been a crispness and energy in Diana's speech and action which
had impressed him favourably.

He did not forget her when he went
to Berg. He did not believe she would
be happy or even comfortable with
the Camphausens, and he often found

himself wondering what she was doing and how she was getting on. He felt that he had had a hand in bringing her to Jacewo, that he was in a measure responsible for her safety and wellbeing while she was there, partly because he was her countryman, the only one of her nation in the place. The feeling that he had some one dependent upon him was new to him, and filled him with an odd pleasure. He enjoyed the feeling for some time, and at the end of a month, made up his mind to go back to Jacewo, and see for himself how she was faring. He had not intended to go so soon; but he told himself that was not at present to the point, and he went as soon as he could.

He reached Jacewo in the evening, and having decided to take the earliest opportunity of paying his respects to Miss Wentworth, he contrived to make a spare half-hour on the following afternoon. He was just pushing open the garden-gate, when the house-door opened, and Frau Camphausen appeared.

She expressed surprise and pleasure at seeing him; and as it never entered into her head that any one not coming to see her husband on business could be calling upon any one but herself, she said at once—

"You see I am going out. I am going to take coffee with Frau Olawska. Will you walk with me so far, and then perhaps you will come in too?"

"Heaven forbid!" thought Garthwaite; but he only said—

"I am going to call on Miss Wentworth, and ask how she is. This is the first opportunity I have had."

The German lady's face and tone changed at once.

"Oh, Miss Wentworth!" she said. "It is unfortunate; but she is out walking with the children."

He felt some surprise, for he knew the ways of the family, and that this was not an hour when it was usual for the children to be out walking.

"Perhaps she may have come in again," he said.

"She has not come in again," frowning, and with a sharp tone in her voice.

"Besides," she went on, "I do not wish Miss Wentworth to have visitors. It will take her mind off her work."

"I see. Has Miss Wentworth many friends here?"

"She knows no one, nor do I think it necessary she should. You are the first person who has asked for her."

"Then you don't think it would be pleasant for her to feel that she has one acquaintance here?"

His tone was calm and mild. Frau Camphausen walked straight into the trap set for her.

"She came to teach, not to enjoy herself; and when I have made a rule, I adhere to it under all circumstances. If you see Miss Wentworth, it will be only in my presence."

"You are really very kind," he said, serenely. "I should be sorry to put you to any inconvenience."

"I am sure you would," with a happy smile; "and as I am very much engaged, it will be better for you not to call on her again. At the same time, I will give her any message you intrust to me."

"Thank you; but I have no message."

"Ah, then I will not mention your coming this afternoon; it might unsettle her."

She had walked on, and Garthwaite was almost obliged to accompany her. He strolled along by her side, continuing

the conversation with his eyes fixed upon
the ground. He was thinking about
Diana; had he looked up at the house,
he would have seen her at an upper
window, looking down upon them. He
did not look up, however, but walked by
Frau Camphausen's side, until she halted,
saying—

"Here we are at Frau Olawska's. Are
you sure you will not come in? she would
be so glad to see you."

He excused himself on the ground that
his half-hour was already at an end, and
went away disappointed that he had not
seen Diana, and glad that he had come
back to look after her. He very much
distrusted the tone in which Frau Camphausen had spoken of her.

When Diana had seen him from the window, she had just left Frau Camphausen, and had come into this room to get a French book from which to read aloud to the girls as they sat at their needlework. She very seldom looked out of the windows, but on this occasion she did draw aside the curtain and look down into the road. The first objects upon which her eyes fell were Frau Camphausen walking slowly along with a man by her side. She saw at once that it must be Mr Garthwaite. His clothing, carriage, and whole appearance proclaimed him an Englishman, and there was only one Englishman at Jacewo. He had come back, then. She bent forward and looked curiously at him. She still could not

see his face, which was turned from her;
but she recognised the general aspect of
his figure, and she saw that he wore the
same heavy fur-lined coat he had had on
the evening of their drive together. She
could see now that he looked well in it.
His tall spare figure carried it with ease,
and a certain distinction which pleased
Diana's fastidious young eyes. She
watched them for a few moments, and
then turned away with an almost imperceptible contraction of her forehead. She
would not confess, even to herself, that
she felt a shade of disappointment at his
having returned to Jacewo, and come
close to the house without having made
any effort to see herself.

A day or two later Minna Camphausen,

the eldest of Diana's pupils, burst into the schoolroom and threw herself into a chair.

"You remember that Englishman who brought you here the night you came?" she said, addressing herself to Diana. "He has come back to Jacewo, and will have supper with us to-night."

"Indeed!" was Diana's reply.

"Yes, he came back a few days ago; and last night papa saw him and asked him to come. He does not often take supper with us; he likes better to drop in in the evening, and sit smoking with papa."

Diana said nothing, and Minna went on—

"Are you not anxious to see him? He

is the only English person who has ever been here except yourself; and his bringing you here was quite romantic—moonlight, too."

"English people see no romance in such a common thing as a gentleman helping a lady out of a difficulty."

"Oh," said Minna, with a toss of her pretty head, "I know you think German girls are always thinking about love-affairs and husbands, and you despise us for it; but we must think of these things. You are only a governess, so it does not matter for you; but mamma is always telling Hedwig and me how careful we must be in the presence of gentlemen, and be sure not to do anything which might make them think us very clever, or fond of books, or used to doing things for ourselves."

"She has not set you a very uncongenial task," was the reply, given with some dryness; but Minna sailed serenely on—

"You know when grandpapa dies we shall have fortunes, and then we shall always have to remember that all these gentlemen who make themselves agreeable to us may be only fortune-hunters, and we must be very careful to whom we speak."

"You are very humble, Minna: it does not seem to occur to you that people may like you for your own sake."

"Oh," said Minna, "that is what you always do — laugh at people and make

them look ridiculous. There is no talking to you with any comfort; I shall go
away."

When Diana was alone again, she put
down her work and thought of the expected guest. She was glad he was
coming; among other reasons, because
she would like to hear English spoken
without this excruciating German accent
which took all the music out of her native
tongue. She felt interested and expec-
tant — the curtain was on the point of
rising, the play was going to begin.

They met in the dining-room; but the
few words of greeting they exchanged
were the only words which passed between
them during supper. Frau Camphausen
took care the conversation should never

fall into their hands, and neither made any effort to frustrate her design. Diana contented herself with studying her compatriot's face. Like him, she could take in a great deal at little more than a glance, and in a short time she was perfectly familiar with Garthwaite's face. She liked it, and the longer she looked at it, the more she liked it. It was not a handsome face, but it was a very characteristic one. The nose and chin were good, clearly cut and well formed, the mouth — scarcely visible under the heavy moustache—closed with great determination; there was a hawk-like keenness and penetration in the iron-grey eyes. It was the face of a man accustomed and naturally fitted to command, yet capable of softening into great tenderness. The head was well set on broad square shoulders, and covered with a mass of dark hair.

After supper they all went into one of the sitting-rooms. The Olawskis came in, and there was promise of a social evening. Both Frau Camphausen and Frau Olawska flirted with Garthwaite; Frau Olawska shamelessly, her friend with moderation, remembering the presence of her daughters and their governess. The Englishman bore it with fortitude; but at the first opportunity he made his way to Diana's side.

" It is a long time since I saw you," he said. " I was obliged to leave Jacewo the day after your arrival, and I have only just come back. I came to call on

you one day, but was told you were
out."

" Which day was that, and what time ? "
holding her needle suspended over her
work as she awaited his answer.

He told her, adding, " Frau Camphausen told me you were out. I met her
just as I reached the house."

" I was in: she knew I was in; I had
but that moment left her ! " she answered,
rather emphatically.

She looked at him as she spoke; he
also looked at her. Their eyes met, and
remained fixed on each other for a moment.

" I suggested that she had made a
mistake," he said.

" I knew you were here," said Diana.
" I saw you with Frau Camphausen."

"Did you think I ought to have called?"

"Yes, I did think so."

"You have a great respect for social observances?"

"I believe they are good."

"And social distinctions, do you believe in them too?"

"I don't think it is wise to penetrate too far into the enemy's country, even if you carry the flag of truce in your hand."

"You would go no further than truce? Perhaps you don't believe in the stability of contracts drawn up under the soothing influence of the pipe of peace. You know tobacco is a very democratic weed."

" You know I dislike it," was her reply, given with a half smile.

" And you believe in the natural enmity of people in different classes? "

" I don't see what they can have in common."

" Ah ! " he said ; " you are young yet."

Frau Olawska had been watching them, devoured with curiosity. She took advantage of the pause which followed Garthwaite's last words, to interrupt with a question of her own.

" Why have you came back to Jacewo so soon? " she asked. " We did not expect you yet."

" I have duties here," he answered, as laconically as Diana herself could have spoken; and although she had no con-

ception of what the duties were to which
he referred, she could not repress a smile
at the very effectual way in which he
silenced the vivacious little Polish lady.

CHAPTER VIII.

NEAR THE FOREST.

SEVERAL days had passed since John had supped at the Camphausens, and he had not seen Diana again. She had excited a strong interest in him, and he was growing impatient for a meeting. Something happened, too, to increase his impatience.

He had come out to post a letter, and having reached the post-office, he pushed his letter into the box. It would not go in; something already filled the slit, and he put his fingers in to discover the cause. He drew out another letter, which had been carelessly posted, and had not dropped into the box; as it came out, with the address side upwards, it was almost unavoidable that he should read it. The envelope was of English paper, and was addressed in an Englishwoman's clear and compact hand, to—

Mrs Wentworth,
    °/₀ Philip Meredith, Esq.,
        The Abbey,
            Garshill,
                Yorks,
                    England.

He held it in his hand for a minute, and then, with a very curious look on his face, looked from it to the letter which he had himself brought to the post, and which was directed to—

```
        Susan Morrison,
            Becktop Farm,
                Garshill,
                    Yorks,
                        England.
```

He looked from one to the other several times, then, smiling to himself, he dropped them both into the letter-box, and went on his way.

The next day he met Diana out of doors, and alone, for she generally took exercise in addition to the morning constitutional with her pupils. She was walking swiftly along the frost - bound road, wrapped in her fur mantle, and with a fur cap set

on her dark hair. Exercise had brought
the warm colour into her cheeks, and her
eyes were brilliantly clear. She was walking along the road to Berg, and had left
the last straggling cottage on the outskirts
of Jacewo some distance behind, being
already within the shadow of the pine-
forest through which the road ran almost
the whole way. The light was on the
point of growing dim, and the flat country
stretched out on either side—visible for
miles without the slightest elevation.
John was going home from the railway,
so met her face to face, and after exchang-
ing greetings, continued his own way
instead of turning back with her.

"Why don't you turn round with me?"
asked Diana at once.

"I have business at Jacewo which is rather pressing. I must get on; and, at the same time, I have something to say to you."

"Then why not say it, and let us each go on our way again? I was enjoying my walk."

"It is too late for you to be out on this road alone. It is never very safe; thieves and cut-throats find it conveniently near the frontier. Berg is under Russian government. You would be exposed to risk at any time, and especially now, with the navvies about."

"Thieves and cut-throats!" she echoed, with a derisive laugh. "Do you seriously expect me to believe in those bogies in the nineteenth century in a civilised country? If thieves and cut-throats are the only dangers to be feared, I will undertake to walk from Jacewo to Berg and back again, without a single qualm of fear."

He heard her out, without being in the least disturbed by her scepticism.

"You talk like a child," he said, when she had done. "They are not only possible but existent. Those woods, which you were on the margin of, extend for miles, and are the shelter of numbers of half-starving men, who will run great risks on the chance of a successful robbery. As for the nineteenth century, and a civilised country, this country is a long way off the nineteenth century, and leaves much to be desired in point of civilisation. You may have noticed as you came along a little mound by the side of the road, with a rough wooden cross at one end. That is the grave of a child who has died since I have been here. Its parents were too poor to provide a funeral and pay the expenses, so they buried the child in that field opposite their cottage."

"I thought it was a dog's grave. But I think they were very wise. Why should they have to pay fees? burying and marrying come in the natural scope of a clergyman's work. Weddings, at least, ought to be performed for love."

He repressed the smile which came on his lips and said—

"Possibly; but you will agree that a country in which such things are done and tolerated, cannot be called a civilised country in our sense of the word, and may permit other things to go on, which would not be suffered in England."

"Oh, well," said Diana, "England is not everywhere, and what's the harm? I should think the child is safer and whole-somer in that field than in the churchyard, where in a year or two his bones would be tossed out of his grave again, to make room for some one else."

John had not enjoyed the privilege of knowing Diana during her childhood, or he would have appreciated this sudden re-version to the tone and phraseology of that happy time. He only smiled and said—

"That last custom stamps the country at once with the seal of the highest civil-isation."

"You are undoubtedly my superior in argument," returned the girl, with a movement of her long throat, which was both graceful and charming in its half-laughing petulance. "Instead of subjecting me to any further defeat, suppose you tell me this wonderful 'thing' which you have in reserve. I can't imagine what you have to say to me, and I am devoured with curiosity to know."

John did not answer at once. A walk with a girl like Diana was a totally new experience to him, and he was surprised to find how much he enjoyed it. So little was he used to walking with women, that it never entered his head to alter his habitual long swinging step when walking by Diana's side; and he was progressing with his usual speed, lost in reflection, instead of attending to what his companion said, when he heard a breathless voice at his side saying—

"How you fly! You remind me of that mythical creature in the nursery rhyme."

"What was that?" stopping short in his walk.

" It was 'a winged beast with teeth and claws.' You first reduce me to mental mince-meat with your superior logic, and then you fly along like an eagle, leaving me to toil after you as I can."

She was half laughing as she finished speaking, and after looking at her for a moment, he too burst out laughing, and they both laughed until they nearly cried.

"Why did you not tell me sooner that

I was going too fast?" he asked, as
they went on again at a more moderate
pace.

"I kept up with you as long as I could.
English people never like to confess themselves beaten, and in this hostile land
one feels inclined to force one's national
characteristics into undue prominence."

"But none of the enemy were by to
see if you had given in."

"Oho!" she answered; "is that the principle on which you are making your railway? But now, tell me what you wanted
to say; you keep putting it off in the
most cunning way. Is it something very
disagreeable, which you don't like to bring
out?"

"That your own conscience must decide

for you. You post your letters very carelessly, Miss Wentworth."

The lightly stepping figure at his side
halted; the   dark   frank   eyes   looked
straight into his as she asked—

"What do you mean?"

He told her what had occurred at the
post-office, and she laughed carelessly, and
asked with some curiosity—

"Which one was it?   I posted three."

He repeated the address to her, and she
said—

"Oh! that — mamma's.   It was of no
importance."

"Suppose it had fallen into the hands
of some unscrupulous person," he said,
with some severity.

"Yes; into Frau Camphausen's hands,

for example. She would have opened and read it. She would have been quite pleased at what was in it."

" Why ? "

" Oh, because I have never given any one a true description of this place. No one wanted me to come, and I would come; so I have always practised a little deception on my friends, and told them how comfortable I am here."

" Are you not comfortable ? " he asked, bluntly.

" Does it strike you as a place in which one would be comfortable ? " she asked, with a little edge in her voice.

" Well, no. To tell the truth, I was rather surprised to find you still here when I came back from Berg."

" Were you ? " she answered. " I am
not going away yet. I don't like the
place, but it interests me a little."

" But to go back to your letter. I
fancied that before you came the Camphausens told me you lived at Whitfield."

" I did ; but when I came here, our
house was broken up and my mother
went to live at Garshill with her brother.
My father had died the year before," she
added, in explanation, for she was in an
expansive mood, which had come upon
her as a sort of reaction from the reserve
she practised towards the Camphausens.

" Is Mr Meredith your mother's brother?"

" Yes ; the only uncle I have."

" Have you ever seen him ? "

" I have never been to his house. I

have never seen him, or any of my cousins. I have four cousins," she concluded, with a laugh which was catching in its melody.

"You seem rather proud of it," he said, with an answering smile.

"I am; as a domestic situation, I believe it is unique," she answered.

There was a pause before John said, in a tone of some constraint—

"Perhaps some day we may be sufficiently intimate for you to tell me about it."

"Would you like to know?" she asked, in a tone of some surprise.

"It would interest me very much indeed," he said, with some emphasis.

"Do you know my uncle?"

"I know him well by repute: I have

seen him. I have relatives who live near Garshill."

" How curious! Well, if I tell you my tale, you must tell me yours; only to make a fair exchange, you know. I am not at all interested in them."

They had entered Jacewo by this time, and had only a few minutes' walk before them. John wondered that she did not ask questions about Garshill. To him it was his native place, the best-loved spot on earth, to which he felt his heart would draw him from the other side of the world. He did not know—forgetting that she had just said she had never seen the place— that the word " Garshill," which always set his heart-strings vibrating, had no special meaning for her. As these thoughts passed through his mind, they reached the Camphausens' house, and were shaking hands. He kept her long slender hand in his as he said—

"Promise me not to walk alone on that road again, Miss Wentworth; I assure you it is not safe."

"Nay;" with the graceful motion of her long throat. "If I promise I shall never rest until I have thoroughly explored it. I shall be safer if you leave me with a warning."

CHAPTER IX.

BY THE LAKE.

For several times after this, John and Diana met only in the presence of the Camphausens, and on these occasions said very little to one another. Frau Camphausen's eagle eye was upon them; for by slow degrees her intelligence had worked round so far as to grasp the fact that, considering the isolated position of these two English people, they must seek each other's society, unless something should happen to render them reciprocally obnoxious. They cared very little for the sanction of her presence, and still less for the supervision of her eagle eye; but without ever having spoken on the subject, there seemed a tacit agreement that, except when alone, they should not converse together for any length of time. So, for some three or four weeks, John had no chance of hearing the explanation of the unique domestic situation which prevailed in Miss Wentworth's family, and Diana on her side had no temptation to lay aside the reserve which characterised her manner with her employers.

After this long time of meeting and yet not meeting, John felt quite a thrill of pleasure when, walking along the street one golden spring afternoon, he saw Diana just before him. He quickened his pace, and soon overtook her and asked whither she was going.

"Nowhere in particular," she answered; "and you?"

"I am going to the railway."

"That is along the road to Berg. Shall we walk together?"

"What are you doing out at this time of day?" asked John, as they strolled along. "I should think every other lady in Jacewo is lying on her sofa fast asleep."

"Yes; I honour and respect that custom of sleeping through the hot part of the day, because I love the heat, and it sets me free to have a walk by myself. They think I am mad, of course, but that does not distress me, and my dress is thin."

He glanced at her dress, and, although he

could not have said why, it produced a feeling of coolness and refreshment in him, and pleased his eye at the same time. It was grey, trimmed with lace and long floating ends of ribbon. Her hat was white, with grey ostrich-feathers curling over its upturned brim; and over her head she held a large parasol of lace, which harmonised with her hat and gown. She stepped lightly under the blazing sun, and her dainty shoes left slight traces of her passing in the dust.

They walked through the town, and passed the cemetery gates and the ruined Polish church; storks flapped lazily through the air, and the windmills creaked and groaned as their sails moved slowly and heavily round; they left behind them the last miserable-looking cottage, with mud floor and thatched roof. The primitive and clumsy combination of pump and well before its door excited the contempt and amusement of the engineer. All this they passed, and then John stood still and said—

"I am not in a hurry, let us go this way : it is a favourite walk of mine, and you may not have seen it."

He turned off the road as he spoke, and went along a rough grass-grown track leading through some fields. The ground dipped a little, so that Diana could not see what was coming, and she uttered a little cry of surprise and delight when she found herself standing on the edge of a vast sheet of water, which stretched before them further than the eye could reach, and lay motionless beneath the blue sky. On the side of the lake on which they stood there ran for a little way a bit of earthen wall, which rose breast-high, and was overgrown with grass and daisies and flowering weeds. Here they came to a standstill, and, leaning their elbows upon it, looked away beyond—

> "Where the long green reed-beds sway
> In the rippled waters grey
> Of that solitary lake"—

to where, in the distance, a patch of sombre pine-trees stood brooding over the still water at their feet.

"I had no idea such a place existed," she said; "I should never have suspected it."

"That is only because you don't know the country. You passed numbers of such lakes, some smaller, some as large or larger, as you came here in the train. This used to be in the midst of the forest, before they cleared the ground."

They stood in silence for a while, then Diana said—

"By the way, since I saw you last, a great event has taken place."

"What is that?"

"They have found a husband for Minna."

"Is that all?"

"All! For heaven's sake don't let them hear you speak like that. It is the event of the day. You know that on the death of their grandfather they will have fortunes, and the choice of a husband in such a case is a very delicate affair."

He caught the infection of her tone

and sparkling eyes, and laughed aloud, asking—

" Well, what is he like ? Have you seen him ? "

" I have seen him."

" What do you think of him ? "

She made a little grimace as she said—

" Oh, as to that, I have not studied him. He is not a gentleman."

He looked at her fixedly for an almost imperceptible time before he asked—

" Ah, that, what do you mean by it ? What kind of gentleman is he not ? "

" Not by birth, not by education, not by mind, not by manners."

" That's tolerably sweeping at all events. You think a great deal of those qualifications ? "

"Why, of course," she answered; "don't you? Life would be impossible without them."

He had noticed before this trick on her part, of throwing a question back upon her interlocutor, and he answered now—

"Oh, my opinion does not matter, at least not at present. I want to have yours. Let's take them in order, as if they were points to be discussed at a con-ference. Birth, now, what's the good of birth?"

"A preliminary to life," was her reply.

"Ah, now," he said, smiling, "don't let us play with words. You know what I mean, and what is the good of birth?"

"Oh," she said, turning her head, for

she saw that he was going to demolish her, " it is useful to know what any one's ancestors have been,—those, for instance, of a baby from whom one is going to be vaccinated."

He laughed outright, but persisted in his catechism—

" But tell me seriously; I have a reason for asking, and want very much to have your opinion. What advantage do you think a man gets from being born of a stock which has always stood well in the world ? "

" Show me first your penny," she answered. " That is, tell me first why you want to know what I think."

" No," he said, immovably. " I won't tell you now ; but I promise I will tell you some time. Will you trust me till I think a fit time has come?"

"Oh yes," was her carelessly given answer. "Why talk so long about nothing? let us get to our points. I do think a man, and a woman too, is better for being born of good stock as you call it. I think it tells. It must help people at difficult points in their lives to remember that if they do wrong they will disgrace not only themselves, but those who went before, and those who will come after."

"That's all theory. When you come to plain fact you find that people think only of themselves and the present; not of what in my part of the country we call their fore-elders, or their descendants at all. Is crime confined to people without ancestry?

I suppose you never heard of kings or dukes, or any such transcendent beings, breaking laws, did you ? "

" Yes; plenty of them," reddening under his tone; " but there will always be exceptions to every rule, and I don't see that they destroy the principle."

" Not now, perhaps," he said, more gently; " but I think you will see it when you are older, and have seen more of life—I think you will then."

" Why do you think so ? " she asked, with some curiosity.

" Because people who don't see it are narrow and selfish, and incapable of all true greatness, and I don't believe you are like that."

She was annoyed to feel that she was

colouring under his fixed gaze, and that she could find no reply to make to him.

"So much for birth," he went on; "as for education—some of the most dastardly men I have known had been educated at our great public schools, and had been at the universities. The most cowardly thing I ever knew done was done by a man belonging to one of the oldest families in England. Manners, too, are only skin-deep, and are often more the result of habitual intercourse with women than the outcome of genuine tenderness and reverence for them. So you see only mind remains; and the longer you live, the more clearly you will see that the only aristocracy is of the mind, the intellect, and the heart, no matter what the birth and education have been. And every man who is a gentleman by nature will have gentle manners, too."

He was rather amazed at himself when he had finished speaking. He had not intended to hold forth like this; but something in Diana's face and attitude, as she listened, had seemed to draw the words from him. The arguments he used, too, were in his estimation so self-evident, he had used them merely because she was clearly such a novice—such a child in her views on these matters. He had spoken simply, that she might easily understand him.

She was silent for a moment, and before she spoke, he went on—

"I suppose you have heard such expressions as 'a born gentleman,' 'a natural gentleman,' used of working men? You see you have to agree with me at last," he said, when she had answered in the affirmative.

"But," she persisted, although she spoke with a little shyness, which became her very well, "we were not considering merely the question of gentlehood. Minna is going to marry this man, and however much a working man might be a gentleman, one could not marry him."

"Why not?"

"Oh!" looking at him with her face full of laughter, as though the idea he had suggested was too ludicrous, "one could not—it would be impossible."

"Not at all. See, the prophet's mantle

has fallen upon me, and I am going to foretell what *might* happen. You yourself, Miss Wentworth, would marry a working man if you thought it desirable."

"Oh no. In what way am I fitted for life in a cottage?"

He looked at her from head to foot before he answered—

"The workman who aspired to marry you would not be content to live in a cottage."

"In what way would he aspire, if I am no higher than he?"

"Because in whatever position you had been born, you would have been a lady, and a lady must always be aspired to."

His face looked very pleasant as he said this. He was smiling at the quick way in which she had taken him up; he was smiling at herself, and yet he spoke earnestly, from his reverence for her.

She met his eyes, and then turned away her head, that she might think of what had been said. All the time she stood thus, with her face turned aside, John's eyes were fixed upon her, and she was keenly conscious that he was looking at her. At length he broke the silence by saying—

"You told me once, Miss Wentworth, that there are peculiarities in your relations with your family, and you said you would explain them to me : will you tell me now?"

"How? Why?" she asked, rather puzzled. "What do you want to know?"

"What induced you to come out to such a remote corner of the world as this?"

"How can the world have corners, if it is round?" she asked; and then went on, "Was it a very extraordinary thing to do?"

"It seems so to me, knowing the place as I do."

"But I did not know the place at all. I came because it was quite strange, and I was tired of everything I knew."

A few more questions from John, and he was in possession of the whole story, with the exception of that part relating to Tom Sherlock. Either she was in a very communicative mood, or John was a very sympathetic listener; at any rate he had the power of drawing her story from her. He listened without speaking, and then said—

"I am glad you did not go; you were right not to go. I sympathise with you entirely."

"I thought you would," she said, showing a confidence in his sympathy and understanding, which he had noticed before.

"And yet these people are perfect strangers to you; possibly if you knew them you might like them."

"Oh no; that is quite impossible. There are four of them—two men and two girls—but I have never seen them."

"Perhaps you will make their acquaintance some time."

"I intend to. I know I am quite different from what they think, and I should like them to know how mistaken they are."

It was the sentiment of a very youthful mind, and John smiled as she spoke.

"Your mother will probably set all that right," he said.

"Oh no; her being there will make very little difference."

He was silent. He knew there were cases of complete want of sympathy between parents and their children. Here was one before his eyes, and he found it very interesting. There was still one test to which he wished to put her; and suddenly changing his tone, he said—

"Now I understand your reluctance to link your lot with a workman, let him be never so chivalrous. It would be against all your family traditions, and you say such things have weight with you. Your people are evidently the great people of the place."

She coloured, and straightened her figure a little. She had been leaning against the earthen wall, plucking daisies and grass and heaping them up, or throwing them down into the water.

"I believe they are," she said with dignity; "but I don't know why you draw attention to it: I have never said such a thing even to myself."

The sun seemed to have left his humour, for he answered—

"There is nothing surprising in that. I should imagine you are very tender with yourself."

She was too angry to speak, and he went on—

"I am interested in these things, and particularly in the fact that I have a member of the English aristocracy before me, because my people are not at all the great people of the place in which they live. They live in a very small way, and have never done anything else. You ought to know it, for you seem to attach great importance to the accident of birth, and I am entirely a self-made man."

His eyes were cold and keen as they met hers, his whole face had changed, and its genial expression had turned into one the very reverse of agreeable. He seemed to be awaiting her reply or counter-remark with almost a sneer upon his lips.

She drew a deep breath as he spoke, and her head was very high as she said—

"You are atrociously rude. Good afternoon."

She walked home without casting one backward glance. She regained the dusty highroad, and walked for some distance along it without encountering any one. The great elm-trees, which met in a lofty arch above her head, whispered and rustled in the breeze; she thought of no one but Garthwaite. She told herself that he was a savage and a boor, and that she could never forgive him. Doubtless his own ancestry, if he had any, had never lifted themselves from the soil, and all his ideas were of the earth, earthy.

CHAPTER X.

" CARISSIMA."

THE conversation which had been brought
to so abrupt a close by Miss Wentworth's
action remained long in the thoughts of
both John and Diana. Now that John
knew her story, who she was, and how
it had come to pass that she was at
Jacewo, his thoughts about her were
strongly tinged with a sort of fierce sarcastic pleasure which was comprehensible
to himself alone. He had heard of parents
and children being antipathetic; he was

himself a case in point, although he never
thought about it or allowed it to influence
him. Here was another and more singular
instance, for the want of sympathy was
between a mother and her only daughter.
From what he had seen of Diana he felt
sure that, charming and sympathetic
though she was to him, many people
might find it difficult or even impossible
to get on with her, and there was really
nothing surprising in the fact that one
such person should be her own mother.
He soon ceased to dwell on that part
of the question; what did arrest his
thoughts, and over and over again bring
into his keen face that look of grim
sarcastic delight, was the story which
Diana had told him, the knowledge of

the family to whom she belonged, the extraordinary fate which had, at any rate for a time, linked her lot with his.

Swinging along the road to Berg, his thoughts ran somewhat in this way—

"So those are her people, and her mother was that Miss Meredith who married that Professor Wentworth. How well I remember the wedding and the village festivities! We were of course forbidden to go near them; but Susan heard of the cakes and goodies, and cried for them, and I said I would get her some. I did, too, and the father found it out and flogged me soundly. I believe Reuben told him," he went on, smiling as he recalled those distant memories. "And that was her mother's wedding! I had forgotten all about it, but how it comes back to me now! I wonder how she would look if I were to tell her. She would be amused and curious, as if her attention had been drawn to the habits of some strange creature from another planet; a little indignant, too, that her kindness and credulity had been imposed upon. Shall I tell her? No; it is no use bringing that ugly light into her eyes, or that spirit into her, when I know she is capable of being brought to see the folly of all that, and I intend to be the man to bring her to it. I intended it before, and these revelations don't in the least alter my mind."

He paused for a moment, and then went on again—

"The very idea of letting a girl such as she is come out here; alone, too! What were they thinking of? It is true they had never seen her, but her mother knew and seems even to have encouraged it. I thought those people always took such care of their women. But to let a girl like Diana Wentworth come out here! The Camphausens dislike her, and if I were not here to look after her, there is no telling what might not happen. I to look after her! There is the cream of the whole affair. Here is a member of the house of Meredith stranded in a remote corner — although the world is round—of semi-civilised Europe, and she owes her comparative comfort and well-being to the fact that she is watched

over by a Garthwaite !" He laughed aloud
at the thought, and in all that great
desert there was no one to hear him; he
could laugh aloud, speak, sing, or cry
aloud, and no one would be the wiser.
There was not a house, or the sign of
a house, within all the range of vision
of his keen long-sighted eyes. " What
would they say if they knew," he continued, "if they knew that one of the
despised race is the guardian angel of the
fairest of their whole fair flock? She is
quite right; as a domestic situation it
is indeed unique, more unique than she
knows. She is not like them. She is
too much unlike them to be thought of
as belonging to them. Suppose I had
been different from what I am, would

she still have talked as frankly to me
and told me her secrets? Suppose I had
been unscrupulous, and had misused my
influence over her — I have some, I believe—would she then have been as frank
and unsuspicious? Suppose I had not
been here at all, but some one else, would
she have been to him what she is to
me? Nay," shaking himself impatiently,
for the thought stung him sharply, "that
is going too far. Besides, if some one
else had been here, she would not have
come. She would have come to wherever
I was. 'Things will be what they will be.'"

Diana was equally thoughtful. Garthwaite's alternate compliments and jeers
stung and thrilled her. The look on
his face when he had said he believed

she was capable of great things, thrilled
her with a feeling she had never known
before, which she only half understood
now. Then the remembrance of the rude
rough words he had said at the last sent
the hot passionate blood in a torrent to
her cheeks. What had made him take
that manner? She alternately wished not
to see him again, and longed impatiently
for a meeting.

She was thinking of these things as she
stood one afternoon alone in the schoolroom. The younger children were still at
school; their parents, with the two elder
girls, were spending the day on the estate
of Herr Platen, the future son - in - law.
After a few days of spring, summer had
come with a burst. It was intensely hot;

the cloudless blue sky was almost fatigu-
ing to look upon, and the sun beat relent-
lessly down upon the thirsty earth; the
air seemed to quiver with the heat. Diana
stood at the window looking out. Before
her the plain stretched out, fringed on the
horizon by a dark line of pine-trees, ten
miles away a tall chimney rose sharply
against the sky, and in all that wide
stretch of country, there was only one
house to be seen. To the left were all the
surroundings of the railway station, and
the railroad to Pawlowsk cut in a straight
line through the plain. A train was coming along, and Diana watched it idly.
She knew by looking at her watch that
it was seven or eight miles distant, yet
she saw the white steam rising clearly

against the blue sky; then the train itself
came in sight, and she wondered who was
in it. She turned her eyes to the trees
growing near the station, and then, taking
some music in her arms, she went down-
stairs to practise.

She felt more inclined to sing than to
play, and she began some old English
airs, which came with peculiar charm and
freshness from her lips.

In the middle of her singing, the front-
door bell rang, and she heard some talking at the door; but she did not cease
singing, and so did not hear that the
visitor, whoever it was, came into the
house, and towards the room where she
sat. She knew nothing until she heard
a voice behind her saying—

"Good afternoon, Miss Wentworth.   I
was very rude to you the last time we
met; will you forgive me?"

She ceased playing, and turned round
quickly.

"How you startled me, Mr Garthwaite!
Is that the tone in which you address your
navvies?"

The meeting, half wished for half avoid-
ed, had come, and she was a little startled
and bewildered.

"I have never had to beg the pardon of
any of my navvies yet," he answered.   "If
I do, I may possibly speak in that tone."

"I am glad you acknowledge that you
were rude."

She had twisted round on the music-
stool, and now sat facing him.

"Of course I acknowledge it," he said. "I was very rude, and I would have followed you at the time to say so; but you walked so fast, I could not overtake you. I thought you would rather not see me again that day."

"You were quite right," she said, somewhat drily.

"You are very angry," he said quickly.

"I *was* very angry," she corrected him; "but to say I am so now, would be to imply that I attach much weight to your opinion, and I do not."

The dignity which always underlay Diana's careless manner was predominant now, and John, who was not overwhelmed by it, looked at her critically as she spoke, and decided that this display became her perfectly. She had risen as she spoke, and the slender white-clad figure looked unusually tall, the beautiful head was held unusually high. John thought her most beautiful as she stood there.

"There is no reason why you should attach much weight to it, if you do not agree with it," he answered, with perfect composure. "Our views on some points differ so widely, that if we were to attach much weight to the opinion of the other, we should be very uncomfortable."

The words were apologetic, the manner was perfectly courteous, and the tone was ironical enough to send the colour into Diana's cheeks. She raised her head even a little higher as she said—

"If I remember rightly, you urged me

for my opinion; it was only your own
which was given unasked."

He had some difficulty in repressing the
smile which trembled on his lips as she
spoke, and he answered hastily—

"Exactly; and it is the fact of mine
having been given unasked which consti-
tutes the rudeness. As an opinion, I had
as much right to it as you had to yours;
there can be no rudeness in the mere
holding of an opinion. But, as you say,
I forced it upon you unasked, which I had
no right to do, and for which I here ask
your pardon."

Diana did not speak at once. His words,
when he had said them, had stung her
very sharply. With time the sting had
grown duller; now that she was reminded

of them, she felt the barb quivering in
her mind once more.

"You *were* rude," she said at last. "I
don't know if I can forgive you."

"See," he answered, "you are angry
still."

It was true; and the weight she had
herself laid upon her anger lasting so long,
returned to her, and made her more angry
still — with this difference, that she was
now as angry with herself as with him.
She knew her colour was rising again, as
he stood with his keen clear eyes fixed
full upon her. She had got herself into
an awkward predicament, and she did not
quite know how to get out of it. It was
difficult after her last words and his to
say anything which should not sound fool-

ish. Perhaps he saw her difficulty, and in his strength was merciful, for he spoke first.

"I promise you," he said, "that it shall not occur again. I see you are not used to contradiction."

He could have taken no surer way to gain his end. Diana almost started as he spoke, and though she did not blush again, she felt her face tingling. He wished her to see that he thought of her as a child. He had begun by treating her as a woman, but he found it would not do; she was too childish and unreasonable. No doubt he would take this as a lesson never to speak seriously to her again, or to take the trouble to dispute her opinions, however foolish they might be. She felt keenly

the degradation of stepping from her position as his friend, to that of the girl with
whom he exchanged a few words from time
to time, because in civility he could not
do less. There was nothing either impulsive or childish in her manner, as she once
more turned to him and said—

"You make too much of it. Pray, say
no more, and let us forget such a trifle."

"With all my heart," he said, a smile
lighting up the depth of his eyes. "Will
you give me your hand, to show we are
friends again?"

She put her hand in his, and he held it
for a moment, looking down at its slender
whiteness: he could have crushed it out of
shape with one squeeze of his own fingers.
Then he loosened his clasp, and said—

"I said I would wait for Herr Camphausen. Will you, in proof of complete
reconciliation, let me wait here, and sing
me something? I heard you singing as
I came in."

"What shall I sing?" she asked, turning
again to the piano; and he replied, "I
leave it to you."

She began without more ado. Her voice
was a contralto of some range, and she
sang with considerable sympathy; it was
always a pleasure to hear her, and John
felt soothed as he listened. He sat by
the side of the piano, turning over her
music, and now and then putting aside
something which he intended to ask her
to sing for him. Presently he came upon
a piece of manuscript music which attract-

ed him more than the others. He held it
in his hand, waiting for her to finish.

She had scarcely taken her fingers from
the keys, before he asked—

"Where did you get this thing?"

"That?" taking it from his hand, and
looking at it. "The words I found in a
novel of Turgenieff's, and the air is an old
German thing, to which they adapted themselves in the most obliging way."

"Sing it for me, will you?" he asked.
"The English, I suppose, is yours."

"Yes," she answered, striking the first
notes.

John did not return to the piano; he
went to the window, and stood in the
shadow of the curtain, looking out. It
was a doleful song she sang, and his heart

grew heavy as he heard it; yet as in a dream, he saw what was passing around him. The work-people were coming from their work in the fields, the women, old and young alike, wearing neither shoes nor stockings, and with gaily coloured handker-chiefs wound round their heads. They were all chatting together in their soft Polish tongue, and snatches of their con-versation came to him through the open window. In a few minutes they had all passed, the road was empty again, and the words of Diana's song came clearly to him, and filled his soul with their haunting melancholy :—

"A heart devoid of joy.

. . . . . .

Love and Grief go hand in hand
In every land, in every land.

.   .   .   .   .   .

> Is anywhere a love to see
> Alike from pain and sorrow free?
> Not anywhere, not anywhere."

His heart ached as he heard her. Was that to be their portion? Would they have to bear and suffer much before all was clear between them? Knowing something of her feelings, could he hope that all ever would be clear between them? He shook off the thought, and when she had finished, went to her side and addressed her in his ordinary manner.

"That song is like your situation — unique," he said.

"Yes; I flattered myself when I found it, that I had come upon something very uncommon."

"Yet, if the song is to be believed, that which it describes is common enough. Is that your opinion?"

"Oh," turning her head aside, "as to that, I cannot judge; I am absolutely without experience.

He had leaned his elbow on the piano, and was looking straight at her as she spoke. His face was serious, and yet he had the air of being amused.

"I do not know whether I am wishing for your happiness if I say, I hope you may never have the experience."

"Oh, surely. Pain and sorrow, and a heart devoid of joy, cannot be desirable."

They were speaking more lightly than they felt, and he went on—

"It depends. There is such a thing

as compensation, and you know there is always a partner in this particular bargain."

"In that case the partner may take the grief and pain and other disagreeables, and I will have the compensation."

He was quite grave again as he said—

"In this bargain the partner *is* the compensation : they cannot be separated."

She would not take her tone from him. She shrugged her shoulders, saying—

"You are getting into too deep water for me, and I will not venture beyond my depth. I can only wade, not swim."

He was going to say more, but she interrupted him with—

"I have never heard you sing, Mr Garthwaite ; can you ?"

"Oh yes, I can sing," he answered, rising to his feet, as if he wished to shake off some unpleasant thought. "Give me your seat for five minutes, and I will show you the best I have to give."

She went to the window, and stood in the shadow of the window-curtain, as he had done, and without any preamble he began to sing "Carissima."

She had never heard it before, and before he had sung many lines, she found herself trembling with excess of feeling, a strange new feeling which had never come to her before. He had a beautiful voice, and the last two lines, with the constant repetition of those two words, "Carissima, carissima," rang in her ears for days afterwards. She suddenly felt

that if John were ever, in a voice like
that, to ask her to do anything for him,
she would find it very difficult to resist
him, let the request be what it might.
When he had finished, she was silent for
a moment, she dared not speak at once,
lest her emotion should betray itself in
her voice. At last she went forward to
the piano, speaking even more lightly than
usual, in her desire not to betray how his
song had moved her.

"Thank you," she said. "That is new
to me; what kind of a song do you call
it? a love-song?"

"Oh no, not a love-song particularly.
It is a song from any man to any
woman."

"I see," she said; "just so," and the

corner of her lips lifted in a half smile. "We won't sing any more, I think," she went on, as he began to screw the music-stool back to her level. "Let us talk instead. I am afraid you will have to wait a long time for Herr Camphausen: they will not be back until evening; they have gone to Herr Platen's estate."

"I will wait a little longer—and that reminds me of something I have wanted to ask you before. Will this approaching marriage make any difference in your arrangements here?"

"No. I had a talk with Frau Camphausen about it, and I agreed to stay on."

"To stay on!" he echoed; "I am surprised. Why stay on?"

"I like the place; I do not want to go."

"You do indeed surprise me," was all he said.

"Why?" she asked, with heightened colour, and a frown on her brow.

"I thought you disliked the place."

"You were mistaken."

"It appears so."

They sat in silence for some time after this. Diana, in her white dress, was the only light object in the sombrely furnished room. John's heart burned within him; she was so very beautiful, so very desirable, he was so sure of his own feelings, so very uncertain, or rather so completely in the dark as to hers. Before he spoke again, a door banged, sounds were heard in the house, feet tramping up-stairs, and loud voices raised in dispute.

"There," said Diana rising, "our talk is at an end. The children have come in from school; I must go to them."

"I am glad we have talked," he said; "because I think we understand each other better now."

"Yes, perhaps," she answered somewhat vaguely, as she gave him her hand.

CHAPTER XI.

GLAMOUR.

IT was dating from this day that Diana began to live in the glamour which surrounded her during the rest of her stay at Jacewo. She and John met nearly every day out of doors, where they were practically, often really, alone. Their meetings were not brought about by appointment—nothing of the kind had ever been even hinted at. They met by attraction: when both were out it seemed inevitable that they should meet, they themselves were passive in the matter. When they were together they talked of everything and anything. Diana told John that she had reason to believe that her letters, if put into the household post-bag, were tampered with before leaving the house. Upon this he took from his watch-chain a little gold seal, and told her to keep it and seal all her letters with it. She refused at first, and seemed to be rather shocked at the idea; but he insisted, and in the end gained his point. The seal now hung from her own watch-chain, its solitary ornament. It had rather a curious device: a globe surmounted by a cross, over which hovered a bat; underneath were the two words "For ever." This seal had an odd

fascination for her; she could not discover
the connection between the device and the
words : it was a shabby little thing, but
she grew fond of it, and later used to
look at it with a queer smile.

Their conversations included some odd
subjects. That is, they might have seemed
odd elsewhere ; here, where everything was
strange, they seemed in keeping with the
surroundings. Sometimes, but very rarely,
John spoke of himself, and it was only after
they had separated that Diana, finding she
could recall every word of those conversations, knew how deeply they had sunk
into her mind.

"It is curious to me to hear you talk
in that way," he said one day, when she
had been ridiculing some want of *savoir*

faire on the part of one of the Jacewo worthies. "You seem to think so much of those things, and in the sense in which you understand the word I am not a gentleman either. I am entirely 'a self-made man.' It does not seem to me that I have any less right to be in the world for that reason, and I should not think it necessary to mention it to any one but yourself; but if I did not tell you, it might possibly make mischief some time. One of these days, if it is ever necessary, I will tell you all about my people; but it is not necessary yet, and unless it were, there is nothing to tell. Mine is not an interesting story like yours. I have no domestic situation."

"Ah," she said, smiling, "you cannot

forget that. I believe you will laugh at me in your own mind as long as you live."

" Well, why shouldn't I ? " he replied; " it does you no harm."

There the subject dropped; she never inquired what he meant by saying he was a self-made man. Either it had no interest for her, or else, he thought, with a smile which his business friends never saw upon his face, " She thinks it would be ill-bred on her part to ask, and might embarrass me to explain."

It was a relief to him that she never asked any questions about her relatives at Garshill. Her indifference was evidently genuine. She never mentioned them, but seemed to have entirely forgotten them. On that one occasion when

they had talked about them, he had forgotten himself and spoken to her in an
unpardonable way. It should never happen again, even were the provocation to
be greater than then. He had not thought
of them for long; when he did, the old
fire blazed up in his heart as fiercely as
ever.

"That song you sang that day," he
began once; "you said you were absolutely without experience. Now I am
not, I have been in love. Once I was
very deeply in love."

Diana turned towards him with her face
full of interest. They were on the edge
of the lake again, leaning against the
earthen wall as they had done on that
other day. Diana happened to wear the

very same clothes : it might have been an exact reproduction of that former scene, but that the sky was a deeper, warmer blue, and the sun sent out a fiercer, more ardent glow. They had been talking and had relapsed into silence; suddenly, after a long pause, John broke out in this way.

"Were you?" she asked. "When was that? Why do you speak as if it were past?"

"It is past; it is all gone, and as though it had never been. I told you once I left home thirteen years ago. I have not been there since. Before I left I asked a girl, with whom I had been in love ever since I was a lad, to marry me. She promised. We plighted our troth with an oath. I did not believe in those things, but she did. She promised to be true to me—to wait till I came back to marry her. I was just beginning. I had my way to make, and the future was uncertain. But she promised, and I left her."

He broke off there, and seemed disinclined to say any more. He had spoken as if under protest, in response to something Diana had said at an earlier stage of their conversation. He would have said no more; but Diana's interest and curiosity had been aroused, and she was bent upon hearing the whole of the story. It was a revelation to her; she had never asked herself any questions about his past life. The past was disregarded as much as the future. She waited some time for him to

go on; but he said nothing, and at last
she asked, with some hesitation—

"And is she waiting yet?"

"No," he answered, "no. Did I not
say it was all at an end?"

"But how?" she persisted. "You should
not have begun, if you did not intend to
tell me the whole of the story."

"Do you care to know? There is really
nothing to tell."

"I care very much," she answered. "Ah!
do tell me."

"It was only like lots of other love-
stories. She found some one whom she
preferred to me."

"Was it a great trouble to you?" she
asked, after a short silence.

"At the time it tried me sorely; now

I have come to see that it was all for the best."

"I wonder if she thinks so too?"

"There I cannot help you," he said, with rather an odd tone in his voice. "I have not seen her again."

"And that is the end of it?"

"That is the end of it."

.   .   .   .   .   .

Little by little she became completely absorbed in her own life. It was far more interesting to her than anything she had ever read, anything she had ever seen on the stage. She did her work faithfully, if mechanically; but she let everything else drift. She gave up writing letters; at intervals of weeks she sent her mother a post-card, or a mere line, and to her

other correspondents she did not send even
that. She scarcely read the letters she got.
These from her mother were empty of all
interest, dealing with persons and things
totally unknown to her, and not to be
weighed against what was going on in
this remote spot of semi-eastern Europe in
which just now she found herself. She did
glance over her mother's letters, scarcely
longer than her own, and no more fre-
quent; but the long epistles she received
from Amy Fairbairn and Tom Sherlock
were tossed into a drawer, generally un-
opened, always unread. Whitfield seemed
like a dim cloud on the horizon of her
memory. What had she to do with it,
or those who lived there? Her past life
there was now like a distant dream, once

vivid, but now faded to a mere misty outline. She kept up a show of correspondence with Mrs Burland, and was from time to time reminded of the existence of her brothers, by seeing their names in some letter which she was skimming with less abstracted eyes than usual. But she had kept her own counsel, she had mentioned John's name to no one. She enjoyed the thought that, except to themselves, their intimacy was unknown; that no one could annoy her with foolish or uncomprehending remarks. She put from her the thought that John and she were not equal. From time to time she was reminded of the fact that he was, as he uncompromisingly called himself, " entirely a self-made man." She turned from it, she refused to heed. She felt that, had she once given serious thought to it, once realised that he was not a gentleman by birth nor made any pretensions to be so, her regard for him must crumble away, their friendship must come to an end. This very feeling, that there was something in their intimacy which she dared not face, gave a zest to the whole affair. She was on the edge of a precipice, the verge of a volcano. She dared not look before her, each step as she took it absorbed all her attention. So she never questioned him, never encouraged him to speak of himself and his past. She shut her eyes resolutely to everything except the present, which held all she wanted. She lived in an ecstasy—rising each day with a feeling that she had awakened in Paradise; and what all this meant, and when or how it was to end, she never asked herself or paused to consider. She took it as it came, feeling only that she had never been so happy in her life, that she had had no conception of what real happiness was.

Perhaps John was equally under a spell. His calm strong manhood had been convulsed. Not even the knowledge of who Diana was, or of the link which existed between them, could destroy the power of her fascination. Had he been asked once, he would have said there could be nothing between them. Before the reality, all that was swept away—to him she was everything in the world. He loved to see her, to hear her talk. He loved to quarrel with her, and become reconciled. He loved her

delicate fastidious tastes and ways, and
her utter childish unreasonableness and
wrong-headedness on many points.   He
loved her as he had never thought to love;
he had made up his mind with his natural
determination that he would win her for
his wife, to love and to cherish till death
should them part.

There were obstacles to be overcome,
and he knew it; but he would not have
been the man he was if the thought of
those obstacles had not been an additional
spur to him,—if the thought that in order
to win her he would have to fight a hard
battle, had not both made her still more
desirable to him, and strengthened his resolution that the victory should be his.

To battle with her people would be

nothing—the thought of it gave him pleasure; but he might have to battle with
herself—and if she was not for him, if
she would not join him, how could he
prevail? There was her love of gentle
birth, her almost unconscious assumption
that nothing less could be tolerated; and
although he had told her more than once
that his own parentage was not up to her
standard, she had always treated him as
a gentleman, as on a level with herself.
What would she say when he told her
that, in the opinion of her world, there
was a huge social gulf between them?
Would her liking survive the shock of
finding that, were they to meet at Garshill, they would stand on totally distinct
social platforms? Had she strength and

faith to put her hand in his, and bridge over that gulf? That was what he wanted to know, that was what he would know. Was a certain dainty flimsiness, which she sometimes took a pleasure in flaunting before him, her real character, all there was of her? Was "her beauty her sole duty," and did it go no deeper than the surface; or was there a true and noble woman underneath? He had his theory, which sooner or later he intended to put to the test.

CHAPTER XII.

IN THE FOREST.

DIANA was walking along the road to Berg. She was alone at home. The whole family, children included, had gone to spend the day on the Platen estate. She herself had been included in the invitation, but Frau Camphausen had not judged fit to transmit the message. She had spent the morning in practising, the afternoon in those vague half - formed thoughts which so often came to her now; and having sipped her cup of coffee and

eaten her supper in all the unusual lux-
ury of solitude, she put on her things
and came out to walk. Almost invol-
untarily her steps turned in the direction of the road to Berg, and she walked
along without noticing how far she was
going. She passed the track leading from
the highroad to the Jacewo lake, she
passed the solitary grave by the roadside, she passed many shrines and crosses,
and still she walked on. She walked
with downcast eyes, for she was thinking
deeply, and she did not notice that she
had got far beyond the point at which
John had once stopped her. Only when
a sudden darkness seemed to fall upon her
path, did she look up and discover that
she was not only in the shadow of the

forest, but had actually walked some little distance in it. She stood still and looked around her. Intense, deepest silence near at hand — and far away, further in the depths of the forest, a swaying sighing sound, which sent a thrill all through her; for what purely natural sound appeals more to the imagination than the wind in pine-trees? She lifted her head and looked on every side — everywhere the same giant trees standing straight and tall, so that she felt a pigmy in their midst. She walked on a few steps, and the sound of her own footsteps startled her. But those few steps had taken her round a bend in the road, and now, looking about her, she saw at some little distance amongst the trees what she took

to be water, one of those lakes of which
John had told her. A strong desire to
get to it came over her; she wanted to
see it close at hand. It did not seem
far away; and even had it been a much
greater distance, her old childish love of
adventure had come over her, and beat
down all objections to her wish. She
vaguely remembered John's warning about
the danger of this forest; but the whole
place exercised a fascination over her
which she could not resist. Besides, she
argued, even if there were robbers in the
forest, they were not likely to be so near
the highroad while it was still broad daylight. She overlooked the facts that
here in the forest it was nothing like
broad daylight any longer, and that the

further she went in the less light it
would be; also, that for a long distance before reaching the forest she had passed no
house anywhere near the roadside. She
silenced all warning, and struck straight
amongst the trees in the direction of
the water. There was no path, it was
difficult to get along, and she soon found
that the lake was further off than she
had expected; but in proportion as her
goal seemed to recede, her determination
to reach it strengthened; and at last,
after so long a struggle that she was
unwilling to think how long a time must
have been occupied in it, she did at last
stand on the shore of the little lake.

No one with an imagination less vivid
than Diana's would have thought it worth

all the trouble it had cost to see. It was very small, and the water was very clear. The pine-trees kept a solemn guard over it, and out of a mass of earth which lay in its midst, grew a tall silver birch-tree. That was all; but Diana stood for a few moments on its brink, and then took out her watch to see how late it might be.

It was later than she had thought, and she thrust it hastily back into her dress. She could not at once find the right place for it, and she still held it in her hand when she turned round to get back to the road. She stopped short, and her hand was arrested in its motion, when she saw a man standing a few paces from her.

It was by no means broad daylight,

but she had no difficulty in seeing the man and distinguishing his features. He was tall, with a thin gaunt figure, and a face with a sullen, rather desperate, expression; his clothing was almost in rags, he looked as though he would hesitate at very little. Still, in spite of his hungry appearance, he looked like an educated man; but Diana only thought he was a robber, and for anything she knew, might have a whole band within call. Even were he alone, she was, as she suddenly recollected, a very long way from help of any kind.

Her heart beat fast, for the encounter was not agreeable, and she stood for a minute looking at him in silence. He spoke first, addressing her in French—

"Will you have the goodness to give me your watch, mademoiselle? You seem to have some difficulty in finding a place for it."

"Thank you," she answered, in a voice which it cost her some effort to keep steady; "I can accommodate my watch perfectly well."

As she spoke she finally deposited it in her dress, and then moved a few steps in the direction of the road.

She had no belief that she would be allowed to escape so easily; and in fact no sooner did she move from the spot on which she had been standing, than two swift steps brought the man in front of her.

"Pardon, mademoiselle," he said again,

"I cannot allow you to pass until you have given me your watch and chain."

He spoke and looked as if he meant what he said; but Diana was naturally fearless, and her anger and spirit were roused by this unceremonious request.

"This is nonsense," she said, with the imperious tone which so often came into her voice when she was thwarted or annoyed; "you must let me pass at once!"

"With pleasure, as soon as ever your watch has passed into my hands."

"I took you for a gentleman at first," she said; "but I see you are nothing but a robber."

The hot temper which had been her bane from childhood was rising, and she scarcely knew what she was saying.

The man shrugged his shoulders as he answered—

"Necessity knows no law; often the mighty are brought low. I should advise you to do what I ask quickly; I should be unwilling to keep you out late."

"You shall not have it," she said, her natural determination coming to her aid. "Let me pass at once. It is cowardly of you to stop a lady who is alone, and to try to frighten her in this way."

"Ah, mademoiselle," he said, "nothing could give me greater pain than to appear at a disadvantage in your eyes. If I seem rough, you must lay it at the door of my unfortunate condition. In short," his tone suddenly changing, "I am starving, and a starving man is desperate.

Give me the watch without more delay, or I must take it by force."

He spoke much more roughly than he had done yet, and Diana bit her lips, and tried to believe that her heart was not beating in a way which almost took away her breath. She began to feel seriously alarmed; but, in spite of her fear, she was cool enough to reason that the loss of her watch and chain, even had she felt no natural disinclination to part with them, could not possibly remain undiscovered and unremarked. Any explanation would be at once awkward and humiliating. Pride urged her to stand out as long as possible. She resolved to try persuasion.

"The watch is of great value to me,"

she said. "It was a gift from my father, who is dead. I cannot believe you would use force against a woman who is alone, and without defence. I beg of you to let me go."

"You shall go as soon as you have done what I ask. I am a gentleman, and without great provocation would not harm a hair of your head. God knows I do not live like this from choice. But the watch I must and will have. If we stay here till midnight, I will not go without it. But the moments are precious, and you must remember you are wholly in my power."

Perhaps with the intention of giving her a gentle reminder of the reality of her position, he came forward a step and laid his hand on her arm. It was a very light touch, but Diana recoiled as if a serpent had darted out its sting at her; everything swam before her eyes, and she trembled from head to foot.

"Oh!" she cried, her voice unsteady with mingled anger and horror, "how dare you touch me! stand back at once!"

She looked desperately round as she spoke, her lips half opened to call for help; and then she closed them again, as the thought came over her, chilling her with sickly fear, that nothing like help was anywhere within reach. She leaned against a tree, scarcely able to stand.

The man, watching her closely, probably saw the effect of his action, and being really desperate, hoped that a repetition of it would bring the scene to a speedy close. He stepped up to her again, and firmly grasping her arm with one hand, with the other seized the wrist of the hand with which she had clutched that part of her dress where she had put her watch.

"Now, mademoiselle!" he said, bringing his face very close to hers.

Her head swam, as she bent it back as far as possible, so as to withdraw her face from his; and she shut her eyes, that she might not see the fierce haggard countenance so near her own. A frantic unreasoning terror took possession of her, and, pushing him from her, she took out the watch, saying with a half sob—

"There! take it and let me go."

His hold relaxed at once, and he seized her watch. The long gold chain was entangled with one of the buttons of her dress, and as she hastily strove to free it, she caught sight of Garthwaite's little shabby seal, which she had forgotten, and which she now suddenly realised was more precious to her than a hundred watches and chains. Her fingers tightened upon it at once, and she said quickly—

"Wait a moment."

"What is it?" he asked, impatiently.

"This little seal; you cannot have it. It is of no value except to me. Let me take it off the chain."

"No, it belongs to me; quick, let me have it."

But she was desperate, with the feeling

that that which she prized most on earth was at stake, that she would endure almost anything rather than let this go; and she returned doggedly—

"No; the watch and chain you may have, but this I will keep."

He might have snatched it from her hand, but he did not, he only said—

"I must have it too. How is it that you attach such price to it, if, as you say, it has no value? Either you are deceiving me, or it is something you prize for its own sake, perhaps a love-token."

Diana's face burned, but she only tightened her hold on the seal without speaking. But her head drooped somewhat, so that she did not see the expression which came into her companion's face. He looked

at her fixedly and in silence for several
moments, and then he said more gently—

"I must request you to give me the
seal."

"No," she said, almost beneath her
breath.

"Then I must take it," beginning to
unclasp her fingers one by one.

He noticed that, in defence of so trum-
pery a thing as this seal, she submitted
to his touch, which had won from her so
valuable an object as her watch. As fast
as he raised her fingers, she closed them
again, with a strength which he had not
believed she possessed. Looking at her
again, he saw that she was very pale, her
lips were compressed, her brows contracted,
her whole face had taken that look of

sternness which did come upon it sometimes. In spite of the sternness she looked
very beautiful, and he said—

"Your faithfulness to this little object
touches me, and I am willing you should
keep it, but on one condition."

"Yes?" she answered, without raising
her eyes.

"The condition is, that you let me kiss
your lips."

"I would rather die."

"Nay," he returned; "not so. And it
is possible that you may have to choose,
because I am determined to have these
things, and I cannot stay here all night."

She was silent, lost in thought. What
was she to do? She was wholly in this
man's power. Help there was none.

Only a robber very sure of his position would have taken this affair as deliberately as this man had done. She could not give up the seal, she would keep it at any price. But such a price! Through her mind flitted the recollection of a duchess, who had bought votes with the price she was asked to pay for this; and what were votes compared with this one gift of her countryman. She made one more effort.

"Name another condition," she said, hurriedly.

"That, and no other," he replied; "and choose at once, or I will take both the things I want."

She drew a long breath, and said—

"I consent; give it to me."

He came nearer to her, bending his
head to hers. She lifted her face; unshed
tears sparkled on her eyelashes, she drew
a long shivering sigh and shut her eyes,
shuddering from head to foot, while she
clenched her fingers upon the seal. She
felt for a second the breath of her persecu-
tor upon her cheek, and then, instead of
coming nearer to her, he suddenly started
away with a loud exclamation, a well-
known voice sounded in her ear, and she
was free.

There was a short parley between Garthwaite and the other man, of which she, in
her surprise and relief and joy, did not
catch one word, and then the man dis-
appeared among the trees, and they were
left standing together.

CHAPTER XIII.

IN DOUBT.

THEY stood for a few minutes, Diana trying to realise that her peril was at an
end; John looking at her with a wrathful
clouded face—such as she had never seen
him wear before. Then he roused himself, and said abruptly, "Come home,"
moving as he spoke in the direction of
the road.

Diana followed him in silence, and it
was not until they were clear of the trees
that she asked—

"How did you find me?"

"You had left this on a thorn, and I went on till I heard voices and saw you."

"This" was a cobwebby handkerchief with "D. W." interlaced in embroidery in one corner. He held it towards her as he spoke; but she merely glanced at it, without offering to take it, so he withdrew it rather hastily, and pushed it into his pocket without saying anything more.

They walked on again in silence, till John, turning again to speak to Diana, saw that she was crying. She was completely unstrung, and utterly unable to keep back her tears. When she saw that John had discovered them, she turned aside her face; but her whole figure shook. Pride, self-control, and all were gone; and she was weeping as John had not thought she could weep.

"Lean on me," he said, gravely. "You are too much upset to walk alone."

She accepted his proffered arm, for indeed she was scarcely able to stand. The strain removed, she began to feel the reaction. Her limbs shook beneath her, and she felt that she could not have walked home alone.

John was silent while her violent fit of sobbing lasted; but by degrees she grew quieter, and before very long, though while they still had a long walk before them, she had withdrawn her hand from his arm, and was speaking in a low tired voice.

"How good of you to come to my rescue!" she said. "This is the second time."

"You are so heedless," he answered, still speaking with unusual gravity. "You need some one to be constantly looking after you; you are not to be trusted alone."

"You have me completely at your mercy," she said, with a tremulous smile. "I cannot defend myself; only remember what Shakespeare says about a giant's strength."

His features relaxed a little. She had a way of taking him which practically disarmed him, and obtained for her very tender treatment indeed.

"Why did you go so far?" he began. "I had warned you; I had told you how dangerous these roads were."

"I had not noticed how far I had got, or I might have turned back sooner."

"If you had kept to the road itself it would not have been so bad; but to positively go right in amongst the trees! It was most foolhardy; and if I had not seen it, I would not have believed that even you could have been so reckless."

"You see you do not know me very well yet," was all her reply.

"I begin to think I do not know you at all."

He spoke with a little bitterness, and as Diana said nothing, there was silence between them until he said—

"Here is your watch."

He spoke abruptly, holding it out, but not looking at her. "In future," he went on, "if you will take these lonely walks, at least leave your valuables at home."

She blushed crimson as she took it from him. She had forgotten all about her watch; and the sight of it, and the little seal dangling from the chain, brought all the past scene vividly before her mind— and for the first time she began to ask herself how much John had seen.

"Thank you," she said, putting it on. "I did not know you had rescued it too. How did you get it? What did you say to that man?" she asked, hesitatingly.

"I told him to make off as fast as he could, or he should be relieved of the responsibility of his maintenance by being placed in prison. If you had not been there, he would have got something a little nearer his deserts."

"You mean you would have knocked

him down, or thrashed him. I am so
glad you did not; I could not bear to see
men fight. How surprised he must have
been to see you!"

"Probably; though, I think, scarcely as
surprised as I was at what I saw, and what
he told me."

Diana was kept silent by a feeling of
guilty confusion which made speech impossible.

"Do you know what I did see?" he
asked.

"I suppose you saw that man and me—
he trying to get possession of my things,
and I doing my best to keep them."

"Yes, I saw that; at least I suppose so.
At first I saw nothing of what you were
holding. I only saw that he was going to

kiss you, and that you were allowing him to do so."

She said nothing: his anger was just; shame and misery kept her silent.

"Was it so? Am I right?" he asked, in a voice which was stern with the effort which he made to keep it calm.

"He would let me keep it on no other terms," she said, forgetting in her wretchedness of what she was speaking, until after the words had left her lips.

"And was it worth such a price?" he asked, with strong scorn; "to barter your maidenly dignity for a paltry watch and chain! Are you *so* fond of finery?"

His words roused her anger, and at the same time caused her keen humiliation; and her reply was prompted by both feelings.

"I set a very high price on them. My father gave them to me years ago, and he is dead."

She spoke with some constraint—tears were not near her eyes now. She had got long past them; she saw one question inevitably coming.

"Even that is not reason enough. But if what that man told me is true, it was not your watch you were going to redeem, but that little seal I gave you. He said you had already yielded the other things. I cannot believe it. Is it true?"

She made no reply; she felt cold all over. What should she say? What could she say?

He waited for a moment, and then, as she said nothing, he repeated—

"Was it so, Diana? Tell me."

His passion would be restrained no longer. It leapt out, and her name came from his lips with an intonation which there could be no mistaking. It thrilled Diana like a chord of music, and in a single second revealed a new world to her startled eyes. She did not speak; she was fighting with herself—torn between two impulses. To tell him he was right would be to confess to him what she had not yet confessed to herself, and to tell him more than he had asked for. To tell him, or let him think the other, would be to not only permit an untruth, but to hopelessly lower herself in his esteem, and kill his regard upon the spot. She did not know what to do. She walked by his side in silence, unheeding that they had by this time reached Jacewo, and totally oblivious of the suspense in which he must be until she spoke. How long she would have halted between two opinions cannot be known, for before she had made up her mind to speak, or with what words she should break the silence, they were accosted by Herr Olawski, who came out of a side-street, and, taking his place by Garthwaite's side, walked on with them.

By this time it was too dark to see Diana's face, and her silence passed unnoticed, as the conversation was chiefly on business. She was both relieved and impatient at the interruption, for she saw there was no chance of any further conversation with John. Herr Olawski lived just beyond the Camphausens, and so would go all the way with them. He did. Garthwaite turned off to his hotel when he reached the main street; only saying, as he shook hands with Diana, "I will see you again, soon," and she concluded her evening walk under the escort of Herr Olawski.

END OF THE FIRST VOLUME.

PRINTED BY WILLIAM BLACKWOOD AND SONS.

CATALOGUE

OF

MESSRS BLACKWOOD & SONS'

PUBLICATIONS.

PHILOSOPHICAL CLASSICS FOR ENGLISH READERS.

EDITED BY WILLIAM KNIGHT, LL.D.,

Professor of Moral Philosophy in the University of St Andrews.

In crown 8vo Volumes, with Portraits, price 3s. 6d.

Now ready—

1. **Descartes.** By Professor MAHAFFY, Dublin.
2. **Butler.** By Rev. W. LUCAS COLLINS, M.A.
3. **Berkeley.** By Professor CAMPBELL FRASER, Edinburgh.
4. **Fichte.** By Professor ADAMSON, Owens College, Manchester.
5. **Kant.** By Professor WALLACE, Oxford.
6. **Hamilton.** By Professor VEITCH, Glasgow.
7. **Hegel.** By Professor EDWARD CAIRD, Glasgow.
8. **Leibniz.** By J. THEODORE MERZ.
9. **Vico.** By Professor FLINT, Edinburgh.
10. **Hobbes.** By Professor CROOM ROBERTSON, London.
11. **Hume.** By the Editor.
12. **Spinoza.** By the Very Rev. Principal CAIRD, Glasgow.
13. **Bacon.** PART I.—The Life. By Professor NICHOL, Glasgow.
14. **Bacon.** PART II.—Philosophy. By the SAME.

Other Vols. in preparation.

FOREIGN CLASSICS FOR ENGLISH READERS.

EDITED BY MRS OLIPHANT.

In crown 8vo, 2s. 6d.

CONTENTS.

DANTE. By the Editor.
VOLTAIRE. By Lieut.-General Sir E. B. Hamley, K.C.B.
PASCAL. By Principal Tulloch.
PETRARCH. By Henry Reeve, C.B.
GOETHE. By A. Hayward, Q.C.
MOLIÈRE. By the Editor and F. Tarver, M.A.
MONTAIGNE. By Rev. W. L. Collins, M.A.
RABELAIS. By Walter Besant, M.A.
CALDERON. By E. J. Hasell.

SAINT SIMON. By Clifton W. Collins, M.A.
CERVANTES. By the Editor.
CORNEILLE AND RACINE. By Henry M. Trollope.
MADAME DE SÉVIGNÉ. By Miss Thackeray.
LA FONTAINE, AND OTHER FRENCH FABULISTS. By Rev. W. Lucas Collins, M.A.
SCHILLER. By James Sime, M.A., Author of 'Lessing: his Life and Writings.'
TASSO. By E. J. Hasell.
ROUSSEAU. By Henry Grey Graham.

NOW COMPLETE.

ANCIENT CLASSICS FOR ENGLISH READERS.

EDITED BY THE REV. W. LUCAS COLLINS, M.A.

Complete in 28 Vols. crown 8vo, cloth, price 2s. 6d. each. And may also be had in 14 Volumes, strongly and neatly bound, with calf or vellum back, £3, 10s.

Saturday Review.—"It is difficult to estimate too highly the value of such a series as this in giving 'English readers' an insight, exact as far as it goes, into those olden times which are so remote and yet to many of us so close."

CATALOGUE

OF

MESSRS BLACKWOOD & SONS'

PUBLICATIONS.

———◆———

ALISON. History of Europe. By Sir ARCHIBALD ALISON, Bart., D.C.L.

1. From the Commencement of the French Revolution to the Battle of Waterloo.
   LIBRARY EDITION, 14 vols., with Portraits. Demy 8vo, £10, 10s.
   ANOTHER EDITION, in 20 vols. crown 8vo, £6.
   PEOPLE'S EDITION, 13 vols. crown 8vo, £2, 11s.

2. Continuation to the Accession of Louis Napoleon.
   LIBRARY EDITION, 8 vols. 8vo, £6, 7s. 6d.
   PEOPLE'S EDITION, 8 vols. crown 8vo, 34s.

3. Epitome of Alison's History of Europe. Twenty-ninth Thousand, 7s. 6d.

4. Atlas to Alison's History of Europe. By A. Keith Johnston.
   LIBRARY EDITION, demy 4to, £3, 3s.
   PEOPLE'S EDITION, 31s. 6d.

——— Life of John Duke of Marlborough. With some Account of his Contemporaries, and of the War of the Succession. Third Edition, 2 vols. 8vo. Portraits and Maps, 30s.

——— Essays: Historical, Political, and Miscellaneous. 3 vols. demy 8vo, 45s.

AIRD. Poetical Works of Thomas Aird. Fifth Edition, with Memoir of the Author by the Rev. JARDINE WALLACE, and Portrait, Crown 8vo, 7s. 6d.

ALLARDYCE. The City of Sunshine. By ALEXANDER ALLARDYCE. Three vols. post 8vo, £1, 5s. 6d.

——— Memoir of the Honourable George Keith Elphinstone, K.B., Viscount Keith of Stonehaven, Marischal, Admiral of the Red. 8vo, with Portrait, Illustrations, and Maps, 21s.

——— Letters from and to Charles Kirkpatrick Sharpe. Edited by ALEX. ALLARDYCE, with a Memoir by the Rev. W. K. R. Bedford. 2 vols. 8vo. Illustrated with Etchings and other Engravings. £2, 12s. 6d.

——— Scotland and Scotsmen in the Eighteenth Century. Edited from the MSS. of John Ramsay, Esq. of Ochtertyre, by ALEX. ALLARDYCE. 2 vols. 8vo, 31s. 6d.

ALMOND. Sermons by a Lay Head-master. By HELY HUTCHIN-
SON ALMOND, M.A. Oxon., Head-master of Loretto School. Crown 8vo, 5s.

ANCIENT CLASSICS FOR ENGLISH READERS. Edited by
Rev. W. LUCAS COLLINS, M.A. Complete in 28 vols., cloth, 2s. 6d. each; or in
14 vols., tastefully bound, with calf or vellum back, £3, 10s.

Contents of the Series.

HOMER: THE ILIAD, by the Editor.—HOMER: THE ODYSSEY, by the Editor.—HER-
ODOTUS, by George C. Swayne, M.A.—XENOPHON, by Sir Alexander Grant, Bart., LL.D.
EURIPIDES, by W. B. Donne—ARISTOPHANES, by the Editor.—PLATO, by Clifton W.
Collins, M.A.—LUCIAN, by the Editor.—ÆSCHYLUS, by the Right Rev. the Bishop of
Colombo.—SOPHOCLES, by Clifton W. Collins, M.A.—HESIOD AND THEOGNIS, by the
Rev. J. Davies, M.A.—GREEK ANTHOLOGY, by Lord Neaves.—VIRGIL, by the Editor.
—HORACE, by Sir Theodore Martin, K.C.B.—JUVENAL, by Edward Walford, M.A.—
PLAUTUS AND TERENCE, by the Editor.—THE COMMENTARIES OF CÆSAR, by Anthony
Trollope.—TACITUS, by W. B. Donne.—CICERO, by the Editor.—PLINY'S LETTERS, by
the Rev. Alfred Church, M.A., and the Rev. W. J. Brodribb, M.A.—LIVY, by the
Editor.—OVID, by the Rev. A. Church, M.A.—CATULLUS, TIBULLUS, AND PROPERTIUS,
by the Rev. Jas. Davies, M.A.—DEMOSTHENES, by the Rev. W. J. Brodribb, M.A.—
ARISTOTLE, by Sir Alexander Grant, Bart., LL.D.—THUCYDIDES, by the Editor.—
LUCRETIUS, by W. H. Mallock, M.A.—PINDAR, by the Rev. F. D. Morice, M.A.

AYTOUN. Lays of the Scottish Cavaliers, and other Poems. By
W. EDMONDSTOUNE AYTOUN, D.C.L., Professor of Rhetoric and Belles-Lettres
in the University of Edinburgh. New Edition, printed from a new type,
and tastefully bound. Fcap. 8vo, 3s. 6d.
Another Edition, being the Thirtieth. Fcap. 8vo, cloth extra, 7s. 6d.
Cheap Edition. Fcap. 8vo. Illustrated Cover. Price 1s.

—— An Illustrated Edition of the Lays of the Scottish Cavaliers.
From designs by Sir NOEL PATON. Small 4to, 21s., in gilt cloth.

—— Bothwell: a Poem. Third Edition. Fcap., 7s. 6d.

—— Poems and Ballads of Goethe. Translated by Professor
AYTOUN and Sir THEODORE MARTIN, K.C.B. Third Edition. Fcap., 6s.

—— Bon Gaultier's Book of Ballads. By the SAME. Fourteenth
and Cheaper Edition. With Illustrations by Doyle, Leech, and Crowquill.
Fcap. 8vo, 5s.

—— The Ballads of Scotland. Edited by Professor AYTOUN.
Fourth Edition. 2 vols. fcap. 8vo, 12s.

—— Memoir of William E. Aytoun, D.C.L. By Sir THEODORE
MARTIN, K C.B. With Portrait. Post 8vo, 12s.

BACH. On Musical Education and Vocal Culture. By ALBERT
B. BACH. Fourth Edition. 8vo, 7s. 6d.

—— The Principles of Singing. A Practical Guide for Vocalists
and Teachers. With Course of Vocal Exercises. Crown 8vo, 6s.

—— The Art of Singing. With Musical Exercises for Young
People. Crown 8vo, 3s.

BALLADS AND POEMS. By MEMBERS OF THE GLASGOW
BALLAD CLUB. Crown 8vo, 7s. 6d

BANNATYNE. Handbook of Republican Institutions in the
United States of America. Based upon Federal and State Laws, and other
reliable sources of information. By DUGALD J. BANNATYNE, Scotch Solicitor,
New York; Member of the Faculty of Procurators, Glasgow. Cr. 8vo, 7s. 6d.

BELLAIRS. The Transvaal War, 1880-81. Edited by Lady BEL-
LAIRS. With a Frontispiece and Map. 8vo, 15s.

—— Gossips with Girls and Maidens, Betrothed and Free.
New Edition. Crown 8vo, 5s.

BESANT. The Revolt of Man. By WALTER BESANT, M.A.
Eighth Edition. Crown 8vo, 3s. 6d.

—— Readings in Rabelais. Crown 8vo, 7s. 6d.

BEVERIDGE. Culross and Tulliallan; or Perthshire on Forth. Its
History and Antiquities. With Elucidations of Scottish Life and Character
from the Burgh and Kirk-Session Records of that District. By DAVID
BEVERIDGE. 2 vols. 8vo, with Illustrations, 42s.

BEVERIDGE. Between the Ochils and the Forth ; or, From Stirling Bridge to Aberdour. By DAVID BEVERIDGE. Crown 8vo, 6s.

BLACK. Heligoland and the Islands of the North Sea. By WILLIAM GEORGE BLACK. Crown 8vo, 4s.

BLACKIE. Lays and Legends of Ancient Greece. By JOHN STUART BLACKIE, Emeritus Professor of Greek in the University of Edinburgh. Second Edition. Fcap. 8vo. 5s.

—— The Wisdom of Goethe. Fcap. 8vo. Cloth, extra gilt, 6s.

—— Scottish Song : Its Wealth, Wisdom, and Social Significance. Crown 8vo. With Music. 7s. 6d.

—— A Song of Heroes. Crown 8vo. [In the press.

BLACKWOOD'S MAGAZINE, from Commencement in 1817 to March 1889. Nos. 1 to 881, forming 144 Volumes.

—— Index to Blackwood's Magazine. Vols. 1 to 50. 8vo, 15s.

—— Tales from Blackwood. Forming Twelve Volumes of Interesting and Amusing Railway Reading. Price One Shilling each, in Paper Cover. Sold separately at all Railway Bookstalls.
They may also be had bound in cloth, 18s., and in half calf, richly gilt, 30s. Or 12 volumes in 6, roxburghe, 21s., and half red morocco, 28s.

—— Tales from Blackwood. New Series. Complete in Twenty-four Shilling Parts. Handsomely bound in 12 vols., cloth, 30s. In leather back, roxburghe style, 37s. 6d. In half calf, gilt, 52s.6d. In half morocco, 55s.

In course of Publication.

—— Tales from Blackwood. Third Series. In Parts. Each price 1s.

In course of Publication.

—— Travel, Adventure, and Sport. From 'Blackwood's Magazine.' In Parts. Uniform with 'Tales from Blackwood.' Each price 1s.

—— Standard Novels. Uniform in size and legibly Printed. Each Novel complete in one volume.

FLORIN SERIES, Illustrated Boards. Or in New Cloth Binding, 2s. 6d.

TOM CRINGLE'S LOG. By Michael Scott.	PEN OWEN. By Dean Hook.
THE CRUISE OF THE MIDGE. By the Same.	ADAM BLAIR. By J. G. Lockhart.
CYRIL THORNTON. By Captain Hamilton.	LADY LEE'S WIDOWHOOD. By General
ANNALS OF THE PARISH. By John Galt.	Sir E. B. Hamley.
THE PROVOST, &c. By John Galt.	SALEM CHAPEL. By Mrs Oliphant.
SIR ANDREW WYLIE. By John Galt.	THE PERPETUAL CURATE. By Mrs Oliphant.
THE ENTAIL. By John Galt.	
MISS MOLLY. By Beatrice May Butt.	MISS MARJORIBANKS. By Mrs Oliphant.
REGINALD DALTON. By J. G. Lockhart.	JOHN : A Love Story. By Mrs Oliphant.

SHILLING SERIES, Illustrated Cover. Or in New Cloth Binding, 1s. 6d.

THE RECTOR, and THE DOCTOR'S FAMILY. By Mrs Oliphant.	SIR FRIZZLE PUMPKIN, NIGHTS AT MESS, &c.
THE LIFE OF MANSIE WAUCH. By D. M. Moir.	THE SUBALTERN.
	LIFE IN THE FAR WEST. By G. F. Ruxton.
PENINSULAR SCENES AND SKETCHES. By F. Hardman.	VALERIUS : A Roman Story. By J. G. Lockhart.

BLACKMORE. The Maid of Sker. By R. D. BLACKMORE, Author of ' Lorna Doone,' &c. New Edition. Crown 8vo, 6s.

BLAIR. History of the Catholic Church of Scotland. From the Introduction of Christianity to the Present Day. By ALPHONS BELLESHEIM, D.D., Canon of Aix-la-Chapelle. Translated, with Notes and Additions, by D. OSWALD HUNTER BLAIR, O.S.B., Monk of Fort Augustus. To be completed in 4 vols. 8vo. Vols. I. and II. 25s.

BOSCOBEL TRACTS. Relating to the Escape of Charles the Second after the Battle of Worcester, and his subsequent Adventures. Edited by J. HUGHES, Esq., A.M. A New Edition, with additional Notes and Illustrations, including Communications from the Rev. R. H. BARHAM, Author of the ' Ingoldsby Legends.' 8vo, with Engravings, 16s.

BROOKE, Life of Sir James, Rajah of Sarāwak. From his Personal Papers and Correspondence. By SPENSER ST JOHN, H.M.'s Minister-Resident and Consul-General Peruvian Republic ; formerly Secretary to the Rajah. With Portrait and a Map. Post 8vo, 12s. 6d.

BROUGHAM. Memoirs of the Life and Times of Henry Lord Brougham. Written by HIMSELF. 3 vols. 8vo, £2, 8s. The Volumes are sold separately, price 16s. each.

BROWN. The Forester : A Practical Treatise on the Planting, Rearing, and General Management of Forest-trees. By JAMES BROWN, LL.D., Inspector of and Reporter on Woods and Forests. Fifth Edition, revised and enlarged. Royal 8vo, with Engravings, 36s.

BROWN. The Ethics of George Eliot's Works. By JOHN CROMBIE BROWN. Fourth Edition. Crown 8vo, 2s. 6d.

BROWN. A Manual of Botany, Anatomical and Physiological. For the Use of Students. By ROBERT BROWN, M.A., Ph.D. Crown 8vo, with numerous Illustrations, 12s. 6d.

BUCHAN. Introductory Text-Book of Meteorology. By ALEXANDER BUCHAN, M.A., F.R.S.E., Secretary of the Scottish Meteorological Society, &c. Crown 8vo, with 8 Coloured Charts and other Engravings, pp. 218. 4s. 6d.

BUCHANAN. The Shirè Highlands (East Central Africa). By JOHN BUCHANAN, Planter at Zomba. Crown 8vo, 5s.

BURBIDGE. Domestic Floriculture, Window Gardening, and Floral Decorations. Being practical directions for the Propagation, Culture, and Arrangement of Plants and Flowers as Domestic Ornaments. By F. W. BURBIDGE. Second Edition. Crown 8vo, with numerous Illustrations, 7s. 6d.

―――― Cultivated Plants : Their Propagation and Improvement. Including Natural and Artificial Hybridisation, Raising from Seed, Cuttings, and Layers, Grafting and Budding, as applied to the Families and Genera in Cultivation. Crown 8vo, with numerous Illustrations, 12s. 6d.

BURTON. The History of Scotland : From Agricola's Invasion to the Extinction of the last Jacobite Insurrection. By JOHN HILL BURTON, D.C.L., Historiographer-Royal for Scotland. New and Enlarged Edition, 8 vols., and Index. Crown 8vo, £3, 3s.

―――― History of the British Empire during the Reign of Queen Anne. In 3 vols. 8vo. 36s.

―――― The Scot Abroad. Third Edition. Crown 8vo, 10s. 6d.

―――― The Book-Hunter. New Edition. With Portrait. Crown 8vo, 7s. 6d.

BUTE. The Roman Breviary : Reformed by Order of the Holy Œcumenical Council of Trent ; Published by Order of Pope St Pius V. ; and Revised by Clement VIII. and Urban VIII. ; together with the Offices since granted. Translated out of Latin into English by JOHN, Marquess of Bute, K.T. In 2 vols. crown 8vo, cloth boards, edges uncut. £2, 2s.

―――― The Altus of St Columba. With a Prose Paraphrase and Notes. In paper cover, 2s. 6d.

BUTLER. Pompeii : Descriptive and Picturesque. By W. BUTLER. Post 8vo, 5s.

BUTT. Miss Molly. By BEATRICE MAY BUTT. Cheap Edition, 2s.

―――― Eugenie. Crown 8vo, 6s. 6d.

―――― Elizabeth, and Other Sketches. Crown 8vo, 6s.

CAIRD. Sermons. By JOHN CAIRD, D.D., Principal of the University of Glasgow. Sixteenth Thousand. Fcap. 8vo, 5s.

―――― Religion in Common Life. A Sermon preached in Crathie Church, October 14, 1855, before Her Majesty the Queen and Prince Albert. Published by Her Majesty's Command. Cheap Edition, 3d.

CAMPBELL. Sermons Preached before the Queen at Balmoral. By the Rev. A. A. CAMPBELL, Minister of Crathie. Published by Command of Her Majesty. Crown 8vo, 4s. 6d.

CAMPBELL. Records of Argyll. Legends, Traditions, and Recollections of Argyllshire Highlanders, collected chiefly from the Gaelic. With Notes on the Antiquity of the Dress, Clan Colours or Tartans of the Highlanders. By LORD ARCHIBALD CAMPBELL. Illustrated with Nineteen full-page Etchings. 4to, printed on hand-made paper, £3, 3s.

CANTON. A Lost Epic, and other Poems. By WILLIAM CANTON. Crown 8vo, 5s.

CAPPON. Victor Hugo. A Memoir and a Study. By JAMES CAPPON, M.A. Post 8vo. 10s. 6d.

CARRICK. Koumiss; or, Fermented Mare's Milk: and its Uses in the Treatment and Cure of Pulmonary Consumption, and other Wasting Diseases. With an Appendix on the best Methods of Fermenting Cow's Milk. By GEORGE L. CARRICK, M.D., L.R.C.S.E. and L.R.C.P.E., Physician to the British Embassy, St Petersburg, &c. Crown 8vo, 10s. 6d.

CAUVIN. A Treasury of the English and German Languages. Compiled from the best Authors and Lexicographers in both Languages. Adapted to the Use of Schools, Students, Travellers, and Men of Business; and forming a Companion to all German-English Dictionaries. By JOSEPH CAUVIN, LL.D. & Ph.D., of the University of Göttingen, &c. Crown 8vo, 7s. 6d.

CAVE-BROWN. Lambeth Palace and its Associations. By J. CAVE-BROWN, M.A., Vicar of Detling, Kent, and for many years Curate of Lambeth Parish Church. With an Introduction by the Archbishop of Canterbury. Second Edition, containing an additional Chapter on Medieval Life in the Old Palaces. 8vo, with Illustrations, 21s.

CHARTERIS. Canonicity; or, Early Testimonies to the Existence and Use of the Books of the New Testament. Based on Kirchhoffer's 'Quellensammlung.' Edited by A. H. CHARTERIS, D.D., Professor of Biblical Criticism in the University of Edinburgh. 8vo, 18s.

CHRISTISON. Life of Sir Robert Christison, Bart., M.D., D.C.L. Oxon., Professor of Medical Jurisprudence in the University of Edinburgh. Edited by his SONS. In two vols. 8vo. Vol. I.—Autobiography. 16s. Vol. II. —Memoirs. 16s.

CHURCH SERVICE SOCIETY. A Book of Common Order: Being Forms of Worship issued by the Church Service Society. Fifth Edition. 6s.

CLOUSTON. Popular Tales and Fictions: their Migrations and Transformations. By W. A. CLOUSTON, Editor of 'Arabian Poetry for English Readers,' 'The Book of Sindibad,' &c. 2 vols. post 8vo, roxburghe binding, 25s.

COCHRAN. A Handy Text-Book of Military Law. Compiled chiefly to assist Officers preparing for Examination; also for all Officers of the Regular and Auxiliary Forces. Specially arranged according to the Syllabus of Subjects of Examination for Promotion, Queen's Regulations, 1883. Comprising also a Synopsis of part of the Army Act. By Major F. COCHRAN, Hampshire Regiment, Garrison Instructor, North British District. Crown 8vo, 7s. 6d.

COLQUHOUN. The Moor and the Loch. Containing Minute Instructions in all Highland Sports, with Wanderings over Crag and Corrie, Flood and Fell. By JOHN COLQUHOUN. Seventh Edition. With Illustrations. Complete in 1 vol. 8vo, 21s.

COTTERILL. Suggested Reforms in Public Schools. By C. C. COTTERILL, M.A., Assistant Master at Fettes College, Edin. Crown 8vo, 3s. 6d.

CRANSTOUN. The Elegies of Albius Tibullus. Translated into English Verse, with Life of the Poet, and Illustrative Notes. By JAMES CRANSTOUN, LL.D., Author of a Translation of 'Catullus.' Crown 8vo, 6s. 6d.

—— The Elegies of Sextus Propertius. Translated into English Verse, with Life of the Poet, and Illustrative Notes. Crown 8vo, 7s. 6d.

CRAWFORD. Saracinesca. By F. MARION CRAWFORD, Author of
'Mr Isaacs,' 'Dr Claudius,' 'Zoroaster,' &c. &c. Fourth Ed. Crown 8vo, 6s.

CRAWFORD. The Doctrine of Holy Scripture respecting the
Atonement. By the late THOMAS J. CRAWFORD, D.D., Professor of Divinity in
the University of Edinburgh. Fourth Edition. 8vo, 12s.

—— The Fatherhood of God, Considered in its General and
Special Aspects, and particularly in relation to the Atonement, with a
Review of Recent Speculations on the Subject. Third Edition, Revised and
Enlarged. 8vo, 9s.

—— The Preaching of the Cross, and other Sermons. 8vo,
7s. 6d.

—— The Mysteries of Christianity. Crown 8vo, 7s. 6d.

CUSHING. The Blacksmith of Voe. A Novel. By PAUL CUSHING,
Author of 'Misogyny and the Maiden,' 'A Woman with a Secret,' &c. 3 vols.
crown 8vo, 25s. 6d.

DAVIES. Norfolk Broads and Rivers; or, The Waterways, Lagoons,
and Decoys of East Anglia. By G. CHRISTOPHER DAVIES, Author of 'The
Swan and her Crew.' Illustrated with Seven full-page Plates. New and
Cheaper Edition. Crown 8vo, 6s.

DAYNE. In the Name of the Tzar. A Novel. By J. BELFORD
DAYNE. Crown 8vo, 6s.

—— Tribute to Satan. A Novel. Crown 8vo, 2s. 6d.

DE LA WARR. An Eastern Cruise in the 'Edeline.' By the
Countess DE LA WARR. In Illustrated Cover. 2s.

DESCARTES. The Method, Meditations, and Principles of Philo-
sophy of Descartes. Translated from the Original French and Latin. With a
New Introductory Essay, Historical and Critical, on the Cartesian Philosophy.
By JOHN VEITCH, LL.D., Professor of Logic and Rhetoric in the University of
Glasgow. A New Edition, being the Ninth. Price 6s. 6d.

DICKSON. Gleanings from Japan. By W. G. DICKSON, Author
of 'Japan: Being a Sketch of its History, Government, and Officers of the
Empire.' In One Volume, with Illustrations. [In the press.

DOBSON. History of the Bassandyne Bible — the First Printed
in Scotland. With Notices of the Early Printers of Edinburgh. By WILLIAM T.
DOBSON, Author of 'Literary Frivolities,' 'Poetical Ingenuities, 'Royal Characters of Scott,' &c. Post 8vo, with Facsimiles and other Illustrations. 7s. 6d.

DOGS, OUR DOMESTICATED: Their Treatment in reference
to Food, Diseases, Habits, Punishment, Accomplishments. By 'MAGENTA.'
Crown 8vo, 2s. 6d.

DU CANE. The Odyssey of Homer, Books I.-XII. Translated into
English Verse. By Sir CHARLES DU CANE, K.C.M.G. 8vo, 10s. 6d.

DUDGEON. History of the Edinburgh or Queen's Regiment
Light Infantry Militia, now 3rd Battalion The Royal Scots; with an
Account of the Origin and Progress of the Militia, and a Brief Sketch of the
old Royal Scots. By Major R. C. DUDGEON, Adjutant 3rd Battalion The Royal
Scots. Post 8vo, with Illustrations, 10s. 6d.

DUNCAN. Manual of the General Acts of Parliament relating to
the Salmon Fisheries of Scotland from 1828 to 1882. By J. BARKER DUNCAN.
Crown 8vo, 5s.

DUNSMORE. Manual of the Law of Scotland as to the Relations
between Agricultural Tenants and their Landlords, Servants, Merchants, and
Bowers. By W. DUNSMORE. 8vo, 7s. 6d.

DUPRÉ. Thoughts on Art, and Autobiographical Memoirs of
Giovanni Duprè. Translated from the Italian by E. M. PERUZZI, with the
permission of the Author. New Edition. With an Introduction by W. W.
STORY. Crown 8vo, 10s. 6d.

ELIOT. George Eliot's Life, Related in her Letters and Journals.
Arranged and Edited by her husband, J. W. CROSS. With Portrait and other
Illustrations. Third Edition. 3 vols. post 8vo, 42s.

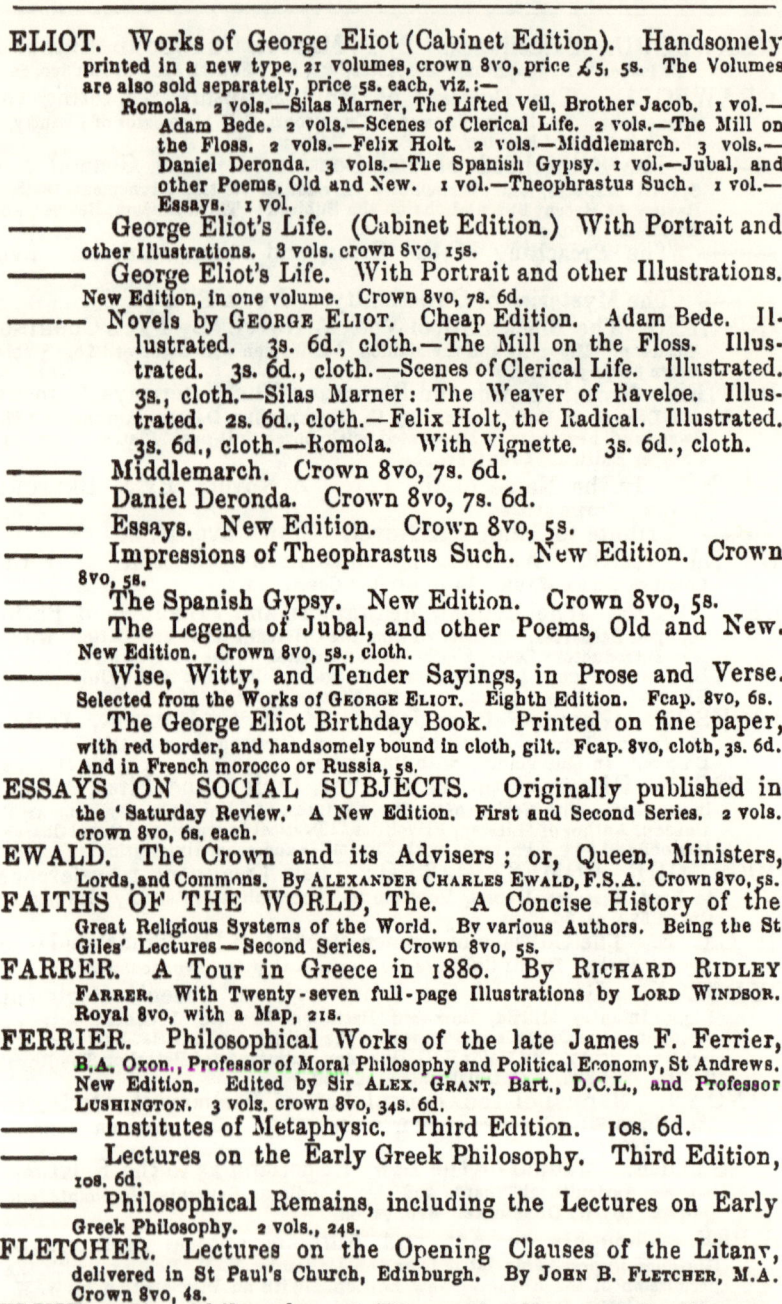

ELIOT. Works of George Eliot (Cabinet Edition). Handsomely printed in a new type, 21 volumes, crown 8vo, price £5, 5s. The Volumes are also sold separately, price 5s. each, viz.:—
Romola. 2 vols.—Silas Marner, The Lifted Veil, Brother Jacob. 1 vol.—Adam Bede. 2 vols.—Scenes of Clerical Life. 2 vols.—The Mill on the Floss. 2 vols.—Felix Holt. 2 vols.—Middlemarch. 3 vols.—Daniel Deronda. 3 vols.—The Spanish Gypsy. 1 vol.—Jubal, and other Poems, Old and New. 1 vol.—Theophrastus Such. 1 vol.—Essays. 1 vol.

———— George Eliot's Life. (Cabinet Edition.) With Portrait and other Illustrations. 3 vols. crown 8vo, 15s.

———— George Eliot's Life. With Portrait and other Illustrations. New Edition, in one volume. Crown 8vo, 7s. 6d.

————— Novels by GEORGE ELIOT. Cheap Edition. Adam Bede. Illustrated. 3s. 6d., cloth.—The Mill on the Floss. Illustrated. 3s. 6d., cloth.—Scenes of Clerical Life. Illustrated. 3s., cloth.—Silas Marner: The Weaver of Raveloe. Illustrated. 2s. 6d., cloth.—Felix Holt, the Radical. Illustrated. 3s. 6d., cloth.—Romola. With Vignette. 3s. 6d., cloth.

———— Middlemarch. Crown 8vo, 7s. 6d.

———— Daniel Deronda. Crown 8vo, 7s. 6d.

———— Essays. New Edition. Crown 8vo, 5s.

———— Impressions of Theophrastus Such. New Edition. Crown 8vo, 5s.

———— The Spanish Gypsy. New Edition. Crown 8vo, 5s.

———— The Legend of Jubal, and other Poems, Old and New. New Edition. Crown 8vo, 5s., cloth.

———— Wise, Witty, and Tender Sayings, in Prose and Verse. Selected from the Works of GEORGE ELIOT. Eighth Edition. Fcap. 8vo, 6s.

———— The George Eliot Birthday Book. Printed on fine paper, with red border, and handsomely bound in cloth, gilt. Fcap. 8vo, cloth, 3s. 6d. And in French morocco or Russia, 5s.

ESSAYS ON SOCIAL SUBJECTS. Originally published in the 'Saturday Review.' A New Edition. First and Second Series. 2 vols. crown 8vo, 6s. each.

EWALD. The Crown and its Advisers; or, Queen, Ministers, Lords, and Commons. By ALEXANDER CHARLES EWALD, F.S.A. Crown 8vo, 5s.

FAITHS OF THE WORLD, The. A Concise History of the Great Religious Systems of the World. By various Authors. Being the St Giles' Lectures—Second Series. Crown 8vo, 5s.

FARRER. A Tour in Greece in 1880. By RICHARD RIDLEY FARRER. With Twenty-seven full-page Illustrations by LORD WINDSOR. Royal 8vo, with a Map, 21s.

FERRIER. Philosophical Works of the late James F. Ferrier, B.A. Oxon., Professor of Moral Philosophy and Political Economy, St Andrews. New Edition. Edited by Sir ALEX. GRANT, Bart., D.C.L., and Professor LUSHINGTON. 3 vols. crown 8vo, 34s. 6d.

———— Institutes of Metaphysic. Third Edition. 10s. 6d.

———— Lectures on the Early Greek Philosophy. Third Edition, 10s. 6d.

———— Philosophical Remains, including the Lectures on Early Greek Philosophy. 2 vols., 24s.

FLETCHER. Lectures on the Opening Clauses of the Litany, delivered in St Paul's Church, Edinburgh. By JOHN B. FLETCHER, M.A. Crown 8vo, 4s.

FLINT. The Philosophy of History in Europe. By ROBERT FLINT, D.D., LL.D., Professor of Divinity, University of Edinburgh. Vol. I. 8vo. [*New Edition in preparation.*

FLINT. Theism. Being the Baird Lecture for 1876. By ROBERT
FLINT, D.D., LL.D., Professor of Divinity, University of Edinburgh. Sixth
Edition. Crown 8vo, 7s. 6d.

—— Anti-Theistic Theories. Being the Baird Lecture for 1877.
Fourth Edition. Crown 8vo, 10s. 6d.

—— Agnosticism. Being the Croall Lectures for 1887-88.
[In the press.

FORBES. Insulinde : Experiences of a Naturalist's Wife in the
Eastern Archipelago. By Mrs H. O. FORBES. Post 8vo, with a Map. 8s. 6d.

FOREIGN CLASSICS FOR ENGLISH READERS. Edited
by Mrs OLIPHANT. Price 2s. 6d. For List of Volumes published, see page 2.

GALT. Annals of the Parish. By JOHN GALT. Fcap. 8vo, 2s.

—— The Provost. Fcap. 8vo, 2s.

—— Sir Andrew Wylie. Fcap. 8vo, 2s.

—— The Entail ; or, The Laird of Grippy. Fcap. 8vo, 2s.

GENERAL ASSEMBLY OF THE CHURCH OF SCOTLAND.

—— Family Prayers. Authorised by the General Assembly of
the Church of Scotland. A New Edition, crown 8vo, in large type, 4s. 6d.
Another Edition, crown 8vo, 2s.

—— Prayers for Social and Family Worship. For the Use of
Soldiers, Sailors, Colonists, and Sojourners in India, and other Persons, at
home and abroad, who are deprived of the ordinary services of a Christian
Ministry. Cheap Edition, 1s. 6d.

—— The Scottish Hymnal Appendix. 1. Longprimer type, 1s.
2. Nonpareil type, cloth limp, 4d.; paper cover, 2d.

—— Scottish Hymnal with Appendix Incorporated. Pub-
lished for Use in Churches by Authority of the General Assembly. 1. Large
type, cloth, red edges, 2s. 6d. ; French morocco, 4s. 2. Bourgeois type, limp
cloth, 1s.; French morocco, 2s. 3. Nonpareil type, cloth, red edges, 6d.;
French morocco, 1s. 4d. 4. Paper covers, 3d. 5. Sunday - School Edition,
paper covers, 1d. 6. Children's Hymnal, paper covers, 1d. No. 1, bound
with the Psalms and Paraphrases, French morocco, 7s. 6d. No. 2, bound
with the Psalms and Paraphrases, cloth, 2s. ; French morocco, 3s.

GERARD. Reata: What's in a Name. By E. D. GERARD.
New Edition. Crown 8vo, 6s.

—— Beggar my Neighbour. New Edition. Crown 8vo, 6s.

—— The Waters of Hercules. New Edition. Crown 8vo, 6s.

—— The Land beyond the Forest. Facts, Figures, and
Fancies from Transylvania. By E. GERARD. In Two Volumes. With Maps
and Illustrations. 25s.

GERARD. Stonyhurst Latin Grammar. By Rev. JOHN GERARD.
Fcap. 8vo, 3s.

GILL. Free Trade : an Inquiry into the Nature of its Operation.
By RICHARD GILL. Crown 8vo, 7s. 6d.

—— Free Trade under Protection. Crown 8vo, 7s. 6d.

GOETHE'S FAUST. Translated into English Verse by Sir THEO-
DORE MARTIN, K.C.B. Part I. Second Edition, post 8vo, 6s. Ninth Edition, fcap., 3s. 6d. Part II. Second Edition, revised. Fcap. 8vo, 6s.

GOETHE. Poems and Ballads of Goethe. Translated by Professor
AYTOUN and Sir THEODORE MARTIN, K.C.B. Third Edition, fcap. 8vo, 6s.

GORDON CUMMING. At Home in Fiji. By C. F. GORDON
CUMMING, Author of 'From the Hebrides to the Himalayas.' Fourth Edition,
post 8vo. With Illustrations and Map. 7s. 6d.

—— A Lady's Cruise in a French Man-of-War. New and
Cheaper Edition. 8vo. With Illustrations and Map. 12s. 6d.

GORDON CUMMING. Fire-Fountains. The Kingdom of Hawaii: Its Volcanoes, and the History of its Missions. By C. F. GORDON CUMMING. With Map and numerous Illustrations. 2 vols. 8vo, 25s.

—— Granite Crags: The Yō-semité Region of California. Illustrated with 8 Engravings. New and Cheaper Edition. 8vo, 8s. 6d.

—— Wanderings in China. New and Cheaper Edition. 8vo, with Illustrations, 10s.

GRAHAM. The Life and Work of Syed Ahmed Khan, C.S.I. By Lieut.-Colonel G. F. I. GRAHAM, B.S.C. 8vo, 14s.

GRANT. Bush-Life in Queensland. By A. C. GRANT. New Edition. Crown 8vo, 6s.

GRIFFITHS. Locked Up. By Major ARTHUR GRIFFITHS. Author of 'The Wrong Road,' 'Chronicles of Newgate,' &c. With Illustrations by C. J. STANILAND, R.I. Crown 8vo, 2s. 6d.

HALDANE. Subtropical Cultivations and Climates. A Handy Book for Planters, Colonists, and Settlers. By R. C. HALDANE. Post 8vo, 9s.

HAMERTON. Wenderholme: A Story of Lancashire and Yorkshire Life. By PHILIP GILBERT HAMERTON, Author of 'A Painter's Camp.' A New Edition. Crown 8vo, 6s.

HAMILTON. Lectures on Metaphysics. By Sir WILLIAM HAMILTON, Bart., Professor of Logic and Metaphysics in the University of Edinburgh. Edited by the Rev. H. L. MANSEL, B.D., LL.D., Dean of St Paul's; and JOHN VEITCH, M.A., Professor of Logic and Rhetoric, Glasgow. Seventh Edition. 2 vols. 8vo, 24s.

—— Lectures on Logic. Edited by the SAME. Third Edition. 2 vols., 24s.

—— Discussions on Philosophy and Literature, Education and University Reform. Third Edition, 8vo, 21s.

—— Memoir of Sir William Hamilton, Bart., Professor of Logic and Metaphysics in the University of Edinburgh. By Professor VEITCH of the University of Glasgow. 8vo, with Portrait, 18s.

—— Sir William Hamilton: The Man and his Philosophy. Two Lectures Delivered before the Edinburgh Philosophical Institution, January and February 1883. By the SAME. Crown 8vo, 2s.

HAMLEY. The Operations of War Explained and Illustrated. By Lieut.-General Sir EDWARD BRUCE HAMLEY, K.C.B., M.P. Fourth Edition, revised throughout. 4to, with numerous Illustrations, 30s.

—— Thomas Carlyle: An Essay. Second Edition. Crown 8vo. 2s. 6d.

—— The Story of the Campaign of Sebastopol. Written in the Camp. With Illustrations drawn in Camp by the Author. 8vo, 21s.

—— On Outposts. Second Edition. 8vo, 2s.

—— Wellington's Career; A Military and Political Summary. Crown 8vo, 2s.

—— Lady Lee's Widowhood. Crown 8vo, 2s. 6d.

—— Our Poor Relations. A Philozoic Essay. With Illustrations, chiefly by Ernest Griset. Crown 8vo, cloth gilt, 3s. 6d.

HAMLEY. Guilty, or Not Guilty? A Tale. By Major-General W. G. HAMLEY, late of the Royal Engineers. New Edition. Crown 8vo, 3s. 6d.

—— Traseaden Hall. "When George the Third was King.' New and Cheaper Edition. Crown 8vo, 6s.

HARBORD. Definitions and Diagrams in Astronomy and Navigation. By the Rev. J. B. HARBORD, M.A., Assistant Director of Education, Admiralty. 1s.

HARRISON. The Scot in Ulster. The Story of the Scottish Settlement in Ulster. By JOHN HARRISON, Author of 'Oure Tounis Colledge.' Crown 8vo, 2s. 6d.

HASELL. Bible Partings. By E. J. HASELL. Crown 8vo, 6s.
——— Short Family Prayers. By Miss HASELL. Cloth, 1s.

HAY. The Works of the Right Rev. Dr George Hay, Bishop of Edinburgh. Edited under the Supervision of the Right Rev. Bishop STRAIN. With Memoir and Portrait of the Author. 5 vols. crown 8vo, bound in extra cloth, £1, 1s. Or, sold separately—viz.:
The Sincere Christian Instructed in the Faith of Christ from the Written Word. 2 vols., 8s.—The Devout Christian Instructed in the Law of Christ from the Written Word. 2 vols, 8s.—The Pious Christian Instructed in the Nature and Practice of the Principal Exercises of Piety. 1 vol., 4s.

HEATLEY. The Horse-Owner's Safeguard. A Handy Medical Guide for every Man who owns a Horse. By G. S. HEATLEY, M.R.C.V.S. Crown 8vo, 5s.
——— The Stock-Owner's Guide. A Handy Medical Treatise for every Man who owns an Ox or a Cow. Crown 8vo, 4s. 6d.

HEMANS. The Poetical Works of Mrs Hemans. Copyright Editions.—One Volume, royal 8vo, 5s.—The Same, with Illustrations engraved on Steel, bound in cloth, gilt edges, 7s. 6d.—Six Volumes in Three, fcap., 12s. 6d. SELECT POEMS OF MRS HEMANS. Fcap., cloth, gilt edges, 3s.

HOME PRAYERS. By Ministers of the Church of Scotland and Members of the Church Service Society. Second Edition. Fcap. 8vo, 3s.

HOMER. The Odyssey. Translated into English Verse in the Spenserian Stanza. By PHILIP STANHOPE WORSLEY. Third Edition, 2 vols. fcap., 12s.
——— The Iliad. Translated by P. S. WORSLEY and Professor CONINGTON. 2 vols. crown 8vo, 21s.

HOSACK. Mary Queen of Scots and Her Accusers. Containing a Variety of Documents never before published. By JOHN HOSACK, Barrister-at-Law. A New and Enlarged Edition, with a Photograph from the Bust on the Tomb in Westminster Abbey. 2 vols. 8vo, £1, 11s. 6d.
——— Mary Stewart. A Brief Statement of the Principal Charges which have been made against her, together with Answers to the same. Crown 8vo, 2s. 6d.

HUTCHINSON. Hints on the Game of Golf. By HORACE G. HUTCHINSON. Fourth Edition. Fcap. 8vo, cloth, 1s. 6d.

IDDESLEIGH. Lectures and Essays. By the late EARL OF IDDESLEIGH, G.C.B., D.C.L., &c. 8vo 16s.

INDEX GEOGRAPHICUS : Being a List, alphabetically arranged, of the Principal Places on the Globe, with the Countries and Subdivisions of the Countries in which they are situated, and their Latitudes and Longitudes. Applicable to all Modern Atlases and Maps. Imperial 8vo, pp. 676, 21s.

JAMIESON. Discussions on the Atonement: Is it Vicarious ? By the Rev. GEORGE JAMIESON, A.M., B.D., D.D., Author of 'Profound Problems in Philosophy and Theology.' 8vo, 16s.

JEAN JAMBON. Our Trip to Blunderland ; or, Grand Excursion to Blundertown and Back. By JEAN JAMBON. With Sixty Illustrations designed by CHARLES DOYLE, engraved by DALZIEL. Fourth Thousand. Handsomely bound in cloth, gilt edges, 6s. 6d. Cheap Edition, cloth, 3s. 6d. In boards, 2s. 6d.

JENNINGS. Mr Gladstone: A Study. By LOUIS J. JENNINGS, M.P., Author of 'Republican Government in the United States,' 'The Croker Memoirs,' &c. Popular Edition. Crown 8vo, 1s.

JERNINGHAM. Reminiscences of an Attaché. By HUBERT E. H. JERNINGHAM. Second Edition. Crown 8vo, 5s.
——— Diane de Breteuille. A Love Story. Crown 8vo, 2s. 6d.

JOHNSTON. The Chemistry of Common Life. By Professor
J. F. W. JOHNSTON. New Edition, Revised, and brought down to date. By
ARTHUR HERBERT CHURCH, M.A. Oxon.; Author of 'Food: its Sources,
Constituents, and Uses:' 'The Laboratory Guide for Agricultural Students;'
'Plain Words about Water,' &c. Illustrated with Maps and 102 Engravings
on Wood. Complete in one volume, crown 8vo, pp. 618, 7s. 6d.

——— Elements of Agricultural Chemistry and Geology. Fourteenth Edition, Revised, and brought down to date. By Sir CHARLES A.
CAMERON, M.D., F.R.C.S.I., &c. Fcap. 8vo, 6s. 6d.

——— Catechism of Agricultural Chemistry and Geology. An
entirely New Edition, revised and enlarged, by Sir CHARLES A. CAMERON,
M.D., F.R.C.S.I.,&c. Eighty-sixth Thousand, with numerous Illustrations, 1s.

JOHNSTON. Patrick Hamilton: a Tragedy of the Reformation
in Scotland, 1528. By T. P. JOHNSTON. Crown 8vo, with Two Etchings by
the Author, 5s.

KENNEDY. Sport, Travel, and Adventures in Newfoundland
and the West Indies. By Captain W. R. KENNEDY, R.N. With Illustrations
by the Author. Post 8vo, 14s.

KING. The Metamorphoses of Ovid. Translated in English Blank
Verse. By HENRY KING, M.A., Fellow of Wadham College, Oxford, and of
the Inner Temple, Barrister-at-Law. Crown 8vo, 10s. 6d.

KINGLAKE. History of the Invasion of the Crimea. By A. W.
KINGLAKE. Cabinet Edition, revised. Illustrated with Maps and Plans. Com-
plete in 9 Vols., crown 8vo, at 6s. each. The Volumes respectively contain:—
I. THE ORIGIN OF THE WAR between the Czar and the Sultan. II. RUSSIA
MET AND INVADED. III. THE BATTLE OF THE ALMA. IV. SEBASTOPOL AT
BAY. V. THE BATTLE OF BALACLAVA. VI. THE BATTLE OF INKERMAN.
VII. WINTER TROUBLES. VIII. and IX. FROM THE MORROW OF INKERMAN
TO THE DEATH OF LORD RAGLAN. With an Index to the Complete Work.

——— History of the Invasion of the Crimea. Demy 8vo. Vol.
VI. Winter Troubles. With a Map, 16s. Vols. VII. and VIII. From the
Morrow of Inkerman to the Death of Lord Raglan. With an Index to the
Whole Work. With Maps and Plans. 28s.

——— Eothen. A New Edition, uniform with the Cabinet Edition
of the 'History of the Invasion of the Crimea,' price 6s.

KNOLLYS. The Elements of Field-Artillery. Designed for the
Use of Infantry and Cavalry Officers. By HENRY KNOLLYS, Captain Royal
Artillery; Author of 'From Sedan to Saarbrück,' Editor of 'Incidents in the
Sepoy War,' &c. With Engravings. Crown 8vo, 7s. 6d.

LADY BLUEBEARD. A Novel. By the Author of 'Zit and
Xoe.' 2 vols. crown 8vo, 17s.

LAING. Select Remains of the Ancient Popular and Romance
Poetry of Scotland. Originally Collected and Edited by DAVID LAING, LL.D.
Re-edited, with Memorial-Introduction, by JOHN SMALL, M.A. With a Por-
trait of Dr Laing. 4to, 25s.

LAVERGNE. The Rural Economy of England, Scotland, and Ireland. By LEONCE DE LAVERGNE. Translated from the French. With Notes
by a Scottish Farmer. 8vo, 12s.

LAWLESS. Hurrish: a Study. By the Hon. EMILY LAWLESS,
Author of 'A Chelsea Householder,' 'A Millionaire's Cousin.' Fourth
and cheaper Edition, crown 8vo, 6s.

LEE. A Phantom Lover: a Fantastic Story. By VERNON LEE.
Crown 8vo, 1s.

LEE. Glimpses in the Twilight. Being various Notes, Records,
and Examples of the Supernatural. By the Rev. GEORGE F. LEE, D.C.L.
Crown 8vo. 8s. 6d.

LEES. A Handbook of Sheriff Court Styles. By J. M. LEES,
M.A., LL.B., Advocate, Sheriff-Substitute of Lanarkshire. New Ed., 8vo, 21s.

——— A Handbook of the Sheriff and Justice of Peace Small
Debt Courts. 8vo, 7s. 6d.

LETTERS FROM THE HIGHLANDS. Reprinted from 'The Times.' Fcap. 8vo, 4s. 6d.

LIGHTFOOT. Studies in Philosophy. By the Rev. J. LIGHTFOOT, M.A., D.Sc., Vicar of Cross Stone, Todmorden. Crown 8vo, 4s. 6d.

LITTLE. Madagascar: Its History and People. By the Rev. H. W. LITTLE, some years Missionary in East Madagascar. Post 8vo, 10s. 6d.

LOCKHART. Doubles and Quits. By LAURENCE W. M. LOCKHART. With Twelve Illustrations. Fourth Edition. Crown 8vo, 6s.

—— Fair to See : a Novel. Eighth Edition. Crown 8vo, 6s.

—— Mine is Thine : a Novel. Eighth Edition. Crown 8vo, 6s.

LORIMER. The Institutes of Law : A Treatise of the Principles of Jurisprudence as determined by Nature. By JAMES LORIMER, Regius Professor of Public Law and of the Law of Nature and Nations in the University of Edinburgh. New Edition, revised throughout, and much enlarged. 8vo, 18s.

—— The Institutes of the Law of Nations. A Treatise of the Jural Relation of Separate Political Communities. In 2 vols. 8vo. Volume I., price 16s. Volume II., price 20s.

M'COMBIE. Cattle and Cattle-Breeders. By WILLIAM M'COMBIE, Tillyfour. New Edition, enlarged, with Memoir of the Author. By JAMES MACDONALD, of the 'Farming World.' Crown 8vo, 3s. 6d.

MACRAE. A Handbook of Deer-Stalking. By ALEXANDER MACRAE, late Forester to Lord Henry Bentinck. With Introduction by HORATIO ROSS, Esq. Fcap. 8vo, with two Photographs from Life. 3s. 6d.

M'CRIE. Works of the Rev. Thomas M'Crie, D.D. Uniform Edition. Four vols. crown 8vo, 24s.

—— Life of John Knox. Containing Illustrations of the History of the Reformation in Scotland. Crown 8vo, 6s. Another Edition, 3s. 6d.

—— Life of Andrew Melville. Containing Illustrations of the Ecclesiastical and Literary History of Scotland in the Sixteenth and Seventeenth Centuries. Crown 8vo, 6s.

—— History of the Progress and Suppression of the Reformation in Italy in the Sixteenth Century. Crown 8vo, 4s.

—— History of the Progress and Suppression of the Reformation in Spain in the Sixteenth Century. Crown 8vo, 3s. 6d.

—— Lectures on the Book of Esther. Fcap. 8vo, 5s.

MACDONALD. A Manual of the Criminal Law (Scotland) Procedure Act, 1887. By NORMAN DORAN MACDONALD. Revised by the LORD JUSTICE CLERK. 8vo, cloth. 10s. 6d.

MACGREGOR. Life and Opinions of Major-General Sir Charles MacGregor, K.C.B., C.S.I., C.I.E, Quartermaster-General of India. From his Letters and Diaries. Edited by LADY MACGREGOR. With Portraits and Maps to illustrate Campaigns in which he was engaged. 2 vols. 8vo, 35s.

M'INTOSH. The Book of the Garden. By CHARLES M'INTOSH, formerly Curator of the Royal Gardens of his Majesty the King of the Belgians, and lately of those of his Grace the Duke of Buccleuch, K.G., at Dalkeith Palace. Two large vols. royal 8vo, embellished with 1350 Engravings. £4, 7s. 6d. Vol. I. On the Formation of Gardens and Construction of Garden Edifices. 776 pages, and 1073 Engravings, £2, 10s.
Vol. II. Practical Gardening. 868 pages, and 279 Engravings, £1, 17s. 6d.

MACINTYRE. Hindu Koh : Wanderings and Wild Sports on and beyond the Himalayas. By Major-General DONALD MACINTYRE, V.C., late Prince of Wales' Own Goorkhas, F.R.G.S. In One Volume, with numerous Illustrations. [In the press.

MACKAY. A Manual of Modern Geography; Mathematical, Physical, and Political. By the Rev. ALEXANDER MACKAY, LL.D., F.R.G.S. 11th Thousand, revised to the present time. Crown 8vo, pp. 688. 7s. 6d.

MACKAY. Elements of Modern Geography. By the Rev. ALEX-
ANDER MACKAY, LL.D., F.R.G.S. 53d Thousand, revised to the present time.
Crown 8vo, pp. 300, 3s.

———— The Intermediate Geography. Intended as an Intermediate Book between the Author's 'Outlines of Geography' and 'Elements of
Geography.' Fourteenth Edition, revised. Crown 8vo, pp. 238, 2s.

———— Outlines of Modern Geography. 181st Thousand, revised to the present time. 18mo, pp. 118, 1s.

———— First Steps in Geography. 105th Thousand. 18mo, pp.
56. Sewed, 4d.; cloth, 6d.

———— Elements of Physiography and Physical Geography.
With Express Reference to the Instructions recently issued by the Science and
Art Department. 30th Thousand, revised. Crown 8vo, 1s. 6d.

———— Facts and Dates; or, the Leading Events in Sacred and
Profane History, and the Principal Facts in the various Physical Sciences.
The Memory being aided throughout by a Simple and Natural Method. For
Schools and Private Reference. New Edition. Crown 8vo, 3s. 6d.

MACKAY. An Old Scots Brigade. Being the History of Mackay's
Regiment, now incorporated with the Royal Scots. With an Appendix containing many Original Documents connected with the History of the Regiment. By JOHN MACKAY (late) OF HERRIESDALE. Crown 8vo, 5s.

MACKAY. The Founders of the American Republic. A History
of Washington, Adams, Jefferson, Franklin, and Madison. With a Supple-
mentary Chapter on the Inherent Causes of the Ultimate Failure of American
Democracy. By CHARLES MACKAY, LL.D. Post 8vo, 10s. 6d.

MACKELLAR. More Leaves from the Journal of a Life in the
Highlands, from 1862 to 1882. Translated into Gaelic by Mrs MARY MACKEL-
LAR. By command of Her Majesty the Queen. Crown 8vo, with Illustrations.
10s. 6d.

MACKENZIE. Studies in Roman Law. With Comparative Views
of the Laws of France, England, and Scotland. By LORD MACKENZIE, one of
the Judges of the Court of Session in Scotland. Sixth Edition, Edited by
JOHN KIRKPATRICK, Esq., M.A. Cantab.; Dr Jur. Heidelb.; LL.B. Edin.;
Advocate. 8vo, 12s.

MAIN. Three Hundred English Sonnets. Chosen and Edited by
DAVID M. MAIN. Fcap. 8vo, 6s.

MAIR. A Digest of Laws and Decisions, Ecclesiastical and Civil,
relating to the Constitution, Practice, and Affairs of the Church of Scotland.
With Notes and Forms of Procedure. By the Rev. WILLIAM MAIR, D.D.,
Minister of the Parish of Earlston. Crown 8vo. With a Supplement, 7s. 9d.

MARMORNE. The Story is told by ADOLPHUS SEGRAVE, the
youngest of three Brothers. Third Edition. Crown 8vo, 6s.

MARSHALL. French Home Life. By FREDERIC MARSHALL.
Second Edition. 5s.

MARSHMAN. History of India. From the Earliest Period to the
Close of the India Company's Government; with an Epitome of Subsequent
Events. By JOHN CLARK MARSHMAN, C.S.I. Abridged from the Author's
larger work. Second Edition, revised. Crown 8vo, with Map, 6s. 6d.

MARTIN. Goethe's Faust. Part I. Translated by Sir THEODORE
MARTIN, K.C.B. Second Ed., crown 8vo, 6s. Ninth Ed., fcap. 8vo, 3s. 6d.

———— Goethe's Faust. Part II. Translated into English Verse.
Second Edition, revised. Fcap. 8vo, 6s.

———— The Works of Horace. Translated into English Verse,
with Life and Notes. 2 vols. New Edition, crown 8vo, 21s.

———— Poems and Ballads of Heinrich Heine. Done into English Verse. Second Edition. Printed on papier vergé, crown 8vo, 8s.

———— Catullus. With Life and Notes. Second Ed., post 8vo, 7s. 6d.

———— Aladdin: A Dramatic Poem. By ADAM OEHLENSCHLAE-
GER. Fcap. 8vo, 5s.

MARTIN. Correggio : A Tragedy. By OEHLENSCHLAEGER. With Notes. Fcap. 8vo, 3s
—— King Rene's Daughter : A Danish Lyrical Drama. By HENRIK HERTZ. Second Edition, fcap., 2s. 6d.

MARTIN. On some of Shakespeare's Female Characters. In a Series of Letters. By HELENA FAUCIT, LADY MARTIN. Dedicated by permission to Her Most Gracious Majesty the Queen. Third Edition. 8vo, with Portrait, 7s. 6d.

MATHESON. Can the Old Faith Live with the New ? or the Problem of Evolution and Revelation. By the Rev. GEORGE MATHESON, D.D. Second Edition. Crown 8vo, 7s. 6d.
—— The Psalmist and the Scientist ; or, Modern Value of the Religious Sentiment. Crown 8vo, 7s. 6d.

MAURICE. The Balance of Military Power in Europe. An Examination of the War Resources of Great Britain and the Continental States. By Colonel MAURICE, R.A., Professor of Military Art and History at the Royal Staff College. Crown 8vo, with a Map. 6s.

MICHEL. A Critical Inquiry into the Scottish Language. With the view of Illustrating the Rise and Progress of Civilisation in Scotland. By FRANCISQUE-MICHEL, F.S.A. Lond. and Scot., Correspondant de l'Institut de France, &c. In One handsome Quarto Volume, printed on hand-made paper, and appropriately bound in Roxburghe style. Price 66s.

MICHIE. The Larch : Being a Practical Treatise on its Culture and General Management. By CHRISTOPHER Y. MICHIE, Forester, Cullen House. Crown 8vo, with Illustrations. New and Cheaper Edition, enlarged, 5s.
—— Practical Forestry. Crown 8vo, with Illustrations. 6s.

MILNE. The Problem of the Churchless and Poor in our Large Towns. With special reference to the Home Mission Work of the Church of Scotland. By the Rev. ROBT. MILNE, M.A., D.D., Ardler. Crown 8vo, 3s. 6d.

MINTO. A Manual of English Prose Literature, Biographical and Critical : designed mainly to show Characteristics of Style. By W. MINTO, M.A., Professor of Logic in the University of Aberdeen. Third Edition, revised. Crown 8vo, 7s. 6d.
—— Characteristics of English Poets, from Chaucer to Shirley. New Edition, revised. Crown 8vo, 7s. 6d.
—— The Crack of Doom. 3 vols. post 8vo, 25s. 6d.

MITCHELL. Biographies of Eminent Soldiers of the last Four Centuries. By Major-General JOHN MITCHELL, Author of 'Life of Wallenstein.' With a Memoir of the Author. 8vo, 9s.

MOIR. Life of Mansie Wauch, Tailor in Dalkeith. With 8 Illustrations on Steel, by the late GEORGE CRUIKSHANK. Crown 8vo, 3s. 6d. Another Edition, fcap. 8vo, 1s. 6d.

MOMERIE. Defects of Modern Christianity, and other Sermons. By the Rev. A. W. MOMERIE, M.A., D.Sc., LL.D., Professor of Logic and Metaphysics in King's College, London. Third Edition. Crown 8vo, 5s.
—— The Basis of Religion. Being an Examination of Natural Religion. Second Edition. Crown 8vo, 2s. 6d.
—— The Origin of Evil, and other Sermons. Fifth Edition, enlarged. Crown 8vo, 5s.
—— Personality. The Beginning and End of Metaphysics, and a Necessary Assumption in all Positive Philosophy. Third Ed. Cr. 8vo, 3s.
—— Agnosticism. Second Edition, Revised. Crown 8vo, 5s.
—— Preaching and Hearing ; and other Sermons. Second Edition. Crown 8vo, 4s. 6d.
—— Belief in God. Second Edition. Crown 8vo, 3s.
—— Inspiration ; and other Sermons. Crown 8vo, 5s.

MONTAGUE. Campaigning in South Africa. Reminiscences of an Officer in 1879. By Captain W. E. MONTAGUE, 94th Regiment, Author of 'Claude Meadowleigh,' &c. 8vo, 10s. 6d.

MONTALEMBERT. Memoir of Count de Montalembert. A Chapter of Recent French History. By Mrs OLIPHANT, Author of the 'Life of Edward Irving,' &c. 2 vols. crown 8vo, £1, 4s.

MURDOCH. Manual of the Law of Insolvency and Bankruptcy : Comprehending a Summary of the Law of Insolvency, Notour Bankruptcy, Composition-contracts, Trust-deeds, Cessios, and Sequestrations; and the Winding-up of Joint-Stock Companies in Scotland; with Annotations on the various Insolvency and Bankruptcy Statutes; and with Forms of Procedure applicable to these Subjects. By JAMES MURDOCH, Member of the Faculty of Procurators in Glasgow. Fifth Edition, Revised and Enlarged, 8vo, £1, 10s.

MY TRIVIAL LIFE AND MISFORTUNE : A Gossip with no Plot in Particular. By A PLAIN WOMAN. New Edition, crown 8vo, 6s.

By the SAME AUTHOR.

POOR NELLIE. New and Cheaper Edition. Crown 8vo, 6s.

NAPIER. The Construction of the Wonderful Canon of Logarithms (Mirifici Logarithmorum Canonis Constructio). By JOHN NAPIER of Merchiston. Translated for the first time, with Notes, and a Catalogue of Napier's Works, by WILLIAM RAE MACDONALD. Small 4to, 15s. *A few large paper copies may be had, printed on Whatman paper, price* 30s.

NEAVES. Songs and Verses, Social and Scientific. By an Old Contributor to 'Maga.' By the Hon. Lord NEAVES. Fifth Ed., fcap. 8vo, 4s.

—— The Greek Anthology. Being Vol. XX. of 'Ancient Classics for English Readers.' Crown 8vo, 2s. 6d.

NICHOLSON. A Manual of Zoology, for the Use of Students. With a General Introduction on the Principles of Zoology. By HENRY ALLEYNE NICHOLSON, M.D., D.Sc., F.L.S., F.G.S., Regius Professor of Natural History in the University of Aberdeen. Seventh Edition, rewritten and enlarged. Post 8vo, pp. 956, with 555 Engravings on Wood, 18s.

—— Text-Book of Zoology, for the Use of Schools. Fourth Edition, enlarged. Crown 8vo, with 188 Engravings on Wood, 7s. 6d.

—— Introductory Text-Book of Zoology, for the Use of Junior Classes. Sixth Edition, revised and enlarged, with 166 Engravings, 3s.

—— Outlines of Natural History, for Beginners ; being Descriptions of a Progressive Series of Zoological Types. Third Edition, with Engravings, 1s. 6d.

—— A Manual of Palæontology, for the Use of Students. With a General Introduction on the Principles of Palæontology. Second Edition. Revised and greatly enlarged. 2 vols. 8vo, with 722 Engravings, £2, 2s.

—— The Ancient Life-History of the Earth. An Outline of the Principles and Leading Facts of Palæontological Science. Crown 8vo, with 276 Engravings, 10s. 6d.

—— On the "Tabulate Corals" of the Palæozoic Period, with Critical Descriptions of Illustrative Species. Illustrated with 15 Lithograph Plates and numerous Engravings. Super-royal 8vo, 21s.

—— Synopsis of the Classification of the Animal Kingdom. 8vo, with 106 Illustrations, 6s.

—— On the Structure and Affinities of the Genus Monticulipora and its Sub-Genera, with Critical Descriptions of Illustrative Species. Illustrated with numerous Engravings on wood and lithographed Plates. Super-royal 8vo, 18s.

NICHOLSON. Communion with Heaven, and other Sermons. By the late MAXWELL NICHOLSON, D.D., Minister of St Stephen's, Edinburgh. Crown 8vo, 5s. 6d.

—— Rest in Jesus. Sixth Edition. Fcap. 8vo, 4s. 6d.

NICHOLSON. A Treatise on Money, and Essays on Present Monetary Problems. By JOSEPH SHIELD NICHOLSON, M.A., D.Sc., Professor of Commercial and Political Economy and Mercantile Law in the University of Edinburgh. 8vo, 10s. 6d.

OLIPHANT. Masollam : a Problem of the Period. A Novel. By LAURENCE OLIPHANT. 3 vols. post 8vo, 25s. 6d.

—— Scientific Religion ; or, Higher Possibilities of Life and Practice through the Operation of Natural Forces. Second Edition. 8vo, 16s.

OLIPHANT. Altiora Peto. By LAURENCE OLIPHANT. New and
Cheaper Edition. Crown 8vo, boards, 2s. 6d. Illustrated Edition. Crown
8vo, cloth, 6s.
—— Piccadilly : A Fragment of Contemporary Biography. With
Eight Illustrations by Richard Doyle. Eighth Edition, 4s. 6d. Cheap Edition,
in paper cover, 2s. 6d.
—— Traits and Travesties ; Social and Political. Post 8vo, 10s. 6d.
—— The Land of Gilead. With Excursions in the Lebanon.
With Illustrations and Maps. Demy 8vo, 21s.
—— The Land of Khemi. Post 8vo, with Illustrations, 10s. 6d.
—— Haifa : Life in Modern Palestine. 2d Edition. 8vo, 7s. 6d.
—— Episodes in a Life of Adventure ; or, Moss from a Rolling
Stone. Fourth Edition. Post 8vo, 6s.
—— Fashionable Philosophy, and other Sketches. In paper
cover, 1s.
—— Sympneumata : or, Evolutionary Functions now Active in
Man. Edited by LAURENCE OLIPHANT. Post 8vo, 10s. 6d.
OLIPHANT. The Story of Valentine ; and his Brother. By Mrs
OLIPHANT. 5s., cloth.
—— Katie Stewart. 2s. 6d.
OSBORN. Narratives of Voyage and Adventure. By Admiral
SHERARD OSBORN, C.B. 3 vols. crown 8vo, 12s.
OSSIAN. The Poems of Ossian in the Original Gaelic. With a
Literal Translation into English, and a Dissertation on the Authenticity of the
Poems. By the Rev. ARCHIBALD CLERK. 2 vols. imperial 8vo, £1, 11s. 6d.
OSWALD. By Fell and Fjord ; or, Scenes and Studies in Iceland.
By E. J. OSWALD. Post 8vo, with Illustrations. 7s. 6d.
OUTCASTS, The ; or, Certain Passages in the Life of a Clergyman.
2 vols. Post 8vo, 17s.
OUTRAM. Lyrics : Legal and Miscellaneous. By the late GEORGE
OUTRAM, Esq., Advocate. New Edition, with Explanatory Notes. Edited
by J. H. Stoddart, LL.D. ; and Illustrated by William Ralston and A. S.
Boyd. Fcap. 8vo, 5s.
PAGE. Introductory Text-Book of Geology. By DAVID PAGE,
LL.D., Professor of Geology in the Durham University of Physical Science,
Newcastle, and Professor LAPWORTH of Mason Science College, Birmingham.
With Engravings and Glossarial Index. Twelfth Edition. Revised and En-
larged. 3s. 6d.
—— Advanced Text-Book of Geology, Descriptive and Indus-
trial. With Engravings, and Glossary of Scientific Terms. Sixth Edition, re-
vised and enlarged, 7s. 6d.
—— Introductory Text-Book of Physical Geography. With
Sketch-Maps and Illustrations. Edited by CHARLES LAPWORTH, LL.D., F.G.S.,
&c., Professor of Geology and Mineralogy in the Mason Science College, Bir-
mingham. 12th Edition. 2s. 6d.
—— Advanced Text-Book of Physical Geography. Third
Edition, Revised and Enlarged by Prof. LAPWORTH. With Engravings. 5s.
PATON. Spindrift. By Sir J. NOEL PATON. Fcap., cloth, 5s.
—— Poems by a Painter. Fcap., cloth, 5s.
PATON. Body and Soul. A Romance in Transcendental Path-
ology. By FREDERICK NOEL PATON. Second Edition. Crown 8vo, 1s.
PATTERSON. Essays in History and Art. By R. HOGARTH
PATTERSON. 8vo, 12s.
—— The New Golden Age, and Influence of the Precious
Metals upon the World. 2 vols. 8vo, 31s. 6d.
PAUL. History of the Royal Company of Archers, the Queen's
Body-Guard for Scotland. By JAMES BALFOUR PAUL, Advocate of the Scottish
Bar. Crown 4to, with Portraits and other Illustrations. £2, 2s.

PEILE. Lawn Tennis as a Game of Skill. With latest revised Laws as played by the Best Clubs. By Captain S. C. F. PEILE, B.S.C. Fourth Edition, fcap. cloth, 1s. 6d.

PETTIGREW. The Handy Book of Bees, and their Profitable Management. By A. PETTIGREW. Fourth Edition, Enlarged, with Engravings. Crown 8vo, 3s. 6d.

PHILOSOPHICAL CLASSICS FOR ENGLISH READERS. Companion Series to Ancient and Foreign Classics for English Readers. Edited by WILLIAM KNIGHT, LL.D., Professor of Moral Philosophy, University of St Andrews. In crown 8vo volumes, with portraits, price 3s. 6d.
[*For list of Volumes published, see page 2.*

POLLOK. The Course of Time : A Poem. By ROBERT POLLOK, A.M. Small fcap. 8vo, cloth gilt, 2s. 6d. The Cottage Edition, 32mo, sewed, 8d. The Same, cloth, gilt edges, 1s. 6d. Another Edition, with Illustrations by Birket Foster and others, fcap., gilt cloth, 3s. 6d., or with edges gilt, 4s.

PORT ROYAL LOGIC. Translated from the French ; with Introduction, Notes, and Appendix. By THOMAS SPENCER BAYNES, LL.D., Professor in the University of St Andrews. Tenth Edition, 12mo, 4s.

POTTS AND DARNELL. Aditus Faciliores : An easy Latin Construing Book, with Complete Vocabulary. By A. W. POTTS, M.A., LL.D., Head-Master of the Fettes College, Edinburgh, and sometime Fellow of St John's College, Cambridge ; and the Rev. C. DARNELL, M.A., Head-Master of Cargilfield Preparatory School, Edinburgh, and late Scholar of Pembroke and Downing Colleges, Cambridge. Tenth Edition, fcap. 8vo, 3s. 6d.

—— Aditus Faciliores Graeci. An easy Greek Construing Book, with Complete Vocabulary. Fourth Edition, fcap. 8vo, 3s.

PRINGLE. The Live-Stock of the Farm. By ROBERT O. PRINGLE. Third Edition. Revised and Edited by JAMES MACDONALD, of the 'Farming World,' &c. Crown 8vo, 7s. 6d.

PUBLIC GENERAL STATUTES AFFECTING SCOTLAND from 1707 to 1847, with Chronological Table and Index. 3 vols. large 8vo, £3, 3s.

PUBLIC GENERAL STATUTES AFFECTING SCOTLAND, COLLECTION OF. Published Annually with General Index.

RAMSAY. Rough Recollections of Military Service and Society. By Lieut.-Col. BALCARRES D. WARDLAW RAMSAY. Two vols. post 8vo, 21s.

RAMSAY. Scotland and Scotsmen in the Eighteenth Century. Edited from the MSS. of JOHN RAMSAY, Esq. of Ochtertyre, by ALEXANDER ALLARDYCE, Author of 'Memoir of Admiral Lord Keith, K.B.,' &c. 2 vols. 8vo, 31s. 6d.

RANKIN. A Handbook of the Church of Scotland. By JAMES RANKIN, D.D., Minister of Muthill ; Author of 'Character Studies in the Old Testament,' &c. An entirely New and much Enlarged Edition. Crown 8vo, with 2 Maps, 7s. 6d.

RANKINE. A Treatise on the Rights and Burdens incident to the Ownership of Lands and other Heritages in Scotland. By JOHN RANKINE M.A., Advocate, Professor of Scots Law in the University of Edinburgh. Second Edition, Revised and Enlarged. 8vo, 45s.

RECORDS OF THE TERCENTENARY FESTIVAL OF THE UNIVERSITY OF EDINBURGH. Celebrated in April 1884. Published under the Sanction of the Senatus Academicus. Large 4to, £2, 12s. 6d.

RICE. Reminiscences of Abraham Lincoln. By Distinguished Men of his Time. Collected and Edited by ALLEN THORNDIKE RICE, Editor of the 'North American Review.' Large 8vo, with Portraits, 21s.

RIMMER. The Early Homes of Prince Albert. By ALFRED RIMMER, Author of 'Our Old Country Towns,' &c. Beautifully Illustrated with Tinted Plates and numerous Engravings on Wood. 8vo, 10s. 6d.

ROBERTSON. Orellana, and other Poems. By J. LOGIE ROBERTSON, M.A. Fcap. 8vo. Printed on hand-made paper. 6s.

—— The White Angel of the Polly Ann, and other Stories. A Book of Fables and Fancies. Fcap. 8vo, 3s. 6d.

—— Our Holiday Among the Hills. By JAMES and JANET LOGIE ROBERTSON. Fcap. 8vo, 3s. 6d.

ROSCOE. Rambles with a Fishing-rod. By E. S. ROSCOE. Crown 8vo, 4s. 6d.

ROSS. Old Scottish Regimental Colours. By ANDREW ROSS, S.S.C., Hon. Secretary Old Scottish Regimental Colours Committee. Dedicated by Special Permission to Her Majesty the Queen. Folio, handsomely bound in cloth, £2, 12s. 6d.

RUSSELL. The Haigs of Bemersyde. A Family History. By JOHN RUSSELL. Large 8vo, with Illustrations. 21s.

RUSSELL. Fragments from Many Tables. Being the Recollections of some Wise and Witty Men and Women. By GEO. RUSSELL. Cr. 8vo, 4s. 6d.

RUSSELL. Essays on Sacred Subjects for General Readers. By the Rev. WILLIAM RUSSELL, M.A. 8vo, 7s. 6d.

RUSTOW. The War for the Rhine Frontier, 1870 : Its Political and Military History. By Col. W. RUSTOW. Translated from the German, by JOHN LAYLAND NEEDHAM, Lieutenant R.M. Artillery. 3 vols. 8vo, with Maps and Plans, £1, 11s. 6d.

RUTLAND. Notes of an Irish Tour in 1846. By the DUKE OF RUTLAND, G.C.B. (Lord JOHN MANNERS). New Edition. Crown 8vo, 2s. 6d.

RUTLAND. Gems of German Poetry. Translated by the DUCHESS OF RUTLAND (Lady JOHN MANNERS). Small quarto, 3s. 6d.

—— Impressions of Bad-Homburg. Comprising a Short Account of the Women's Associations of Germany under the Red Cross. Crown 8vo, 1s. 6d.

—— Some Personal Recollections of the Later Years of the Earl of Beaconsfield, K.G. Sixth Edition, 6d.

—— Employment of Women in the Public Service. 6d.

—— Some of the Advantages of Easily Accessible Reading and Recreation Rooms, and Free Libraries. With Remarks on Starting and Maintaining Them. Second Edition, crown 8vo, 1s.

—— A Sequel to Rich Men's Dwellings, and other Occasional Papers. Crown 8vo, 2s. 6d.

—— Encouraging Experiences of Reading and Recreation Rooms. Aims of Guilds, Nottingham Social Guild, Existing Institutions, &c., &c. Crown 8vo, 1s.

SCHILLER. Wallenstein. A Dramatic Poem. By FREDERICK VON SCHILLER. Translated by C. G. A. LOCKHART. Fcap. 8vo, 7s. 6d.

SCOTCH LOCH FISHING. By "Black Palmer." Crown 8vo, interleaved with blank pages, 4s.

SELLAR. Manual of the Education Acts for Scotland. By ALEXANDER CRAIG SELLAR, M.P. Eighth Edition. Revised and in great part rewritten by J. EDWARD GRAHAM, B.A. Oxon., Advocate. Containing the Technical Schools Act, 1887, and all Acts bearing on Education in Scotland. With Rules for the conduct of Elections, with Notes and Cases. 8vo, 10s. 6d.

SELLER AND STEPHENS. Physiology at the Farm ; in Aid of Rearing and Feeding the Live Stock. By WILLIAM SELLER, M.D., F.R.S.E., and HENRY STEPHENS, F.R.S.E., Author of 'The Book of the Farm,' &c. Post 8vo, with Engravings, 16s.

SETH. Scottish Philosophy. A Comparison of the Scottish and German Answers to Hume. Balfour Philosophical Lectures, University of Edinburgh. By ANDREW SETH, M.A., Professor of Logic, Rhetoric, and Metaphysics in the University of St Andrews. Crown 8vo, 5s.

—— Hegelianism and Personality. Balfour Philosophical Lectures. Second Series. Crown 8vo, 5s.

SETON. A Budget of Anecdotes. Chiefly relating to the Current Century. Compiled and Arranged by GEORGE SETON, Advocate, M.A. Oxon. New and Cheaper Edition, fcap. 8vo. Boards, 1s. 6d.

SHADWELL. The Life of Colin Campbell, Lord Clyde. Illustrated by Extracts from his Diary and Correspondence. By Lieutenant-General SHADWELL, C.B. 2 vols. 8vo. With Portrait, Maps, and Plans. 36s.

SHAND. Half a Century; or, Changes in Men and Manners. By ALEX. INNES SHAND, Author of 'Against Time,' &c. Second Ed., 8vo, 12s. 6d.

—— Letters from the West of Ireland. Reprinted from the 'Times.' Crown 8vo, 5s.

SHARPE. Letters from and to Charles Kirkpatrick Sharpe. Edited by ALEXANDER ALLARDYCE, Author of 'Memoir of Admiral Lord Keith, K.B.,' &c. With a Memoir by the Rev. W. K. R. BEDFORD. In two vols. 8vo. Illustrated with Etchings and other Engravings. £2, 12s. 6d.

SIM. Margaret Sim's Cookery. With an Introduction by L. B. WALFORD, Author of 'Mr Smith: A Part of His Life,' &c. Crown 8vo, 5s.

SKELTON. Maitland of Lethington; and the Scotland of Mary Stuart. A History. By JOHN SKELTON, C.B., LL.D. Author of 'The Essays of Shirley.' Demy 8vo. 2 vols., 28s.

SMITH. Italian Irrigation: A Report on the Agricultural Canals of Piedmont and Lombardy, addressed to the Hon. the Directors of the East India Company; with an Appendix, containing a Sketch of the Irrigation System of Northern and Central India. By Lieut.-Col. R. BAIRD SMITH, F.G.S., Bengal Engineers. Second Edition. 2 vols. 8vo, with Atlas, 30s.

SMITH. Thorndale; or, The Conflict of Opinions. By WILLIAM SMITH, Author of 'A Discourse on Ethics,' &c. New Edition. Cr. 8vo, 10s. 6d.

—— Gravenhurst; or, Thoughts on Good and Evil. Second Edition, with Memoir of the Author. Crown 8vo, 8s.

SMITH. Greek Testament Lessons for Colleges, Schools, and Private Students, consisting chiefly of the Sermon on the Mount and the Parables of our Lord. With Notes and Essays. By the Rev. J. HUNTER SMITH, M.A., King Edward's School, Birmingham. Crown 8vo, 6s.

SMITH. Writings by the Way. By JOHN CAMPBELL SMITH, M.A., Sheriff-Substitute. Crown 8vo, 9s.

SMITH. The Secretary for Scotland. Being a Statement of the Powers and Duties of the new Scottish Office. With a Short Historical Introduction and numerous references to important Administrative Documents. By W. C. SMITH, LL.B., Advocate. 8vo, 6s.

SOLTERA. A Lady's Ride Across Spanish Honduras. By MARIA SOLTERA. With Illustrations. Post 8vo, 12s. 6d.

—— The Fat of the Land. A Novel. 3 vols. post 8vo, 25s. 6d.

SORLEY. The Ethics of Naturalism. Being the Shaw Fellowship Lectures, 1884. By W. R. Sorley, M.A., Fellow of Trinity College, Cambridge, and Examiner in Philosophy in the University of Edinburgh. Crown 8vo, 6s.

SPEEDY. Sport in the Highlands and Lowlands of Scotland with Rod and Gun. By TOM SPEEDY. Second Edition, Revised and Enlarged. With Illustrations by Lieut.-Gen. Hope Crealocke, C.B., C.M.G., and others. 8vo, 15s.

SPROTT. The Worship and Offices of the Church of Scotland. By GEORGE W. SPROTT, D.D., Minister of North Berwick. Crown 8vo, 6s.

STARFORTH. Villa Residences and Farm Architecture : A Series of Designs. By JOHN STARFORTH, Architect. 102 Engravings. Second Edition, medium 4to, £2, 17s. 6d.

STATISTICAL ACCOUNT OF SCOTLAND. Complete, with Index, 15 vols. 8vo, £16, 16s. Each County sold separately, with Title, Index, and Map, neatly bound in cloth, forming a very valuable Manual to the Landowner, the Tenant, the Manufacturer, the Naturalist, the Tourist, &c.

In course of publication.

STEPHENS' BOOK OF THE FARM; detailing the Labours of the Farmer, Farm-Steward, Ploughman, Shepherd, Hedger, Farm-Labourer, Field-Worker, and Cattleman. Illustrated with numerous Portraits of Animals and Engravings of Implements. Fourth Edition. Revised, and in great part rewritten by JAMES MACDONALD, of the 'Farming World,' &c., &c. Assisted by many of the leading agricultural authorities of the day. To be completed in Six Divisional Volumes.

[*Divisions I. and II., price 10s. 6d. each, now ready.*

STEPHENS. The Book of Farm Buildings; their Arrangement and Construction. By HENRY STEPHENS, F.R.S.E., Author of 'The Book of the Farm;' and ROBERT SCOTT BURN. Illustrated with 1045 Plates and Engravings. Large 8vo, uniform with 'The Book of the Farm,' &c. £1, 11s. 6d.

—— The Book of Farm Implements and Machines. By J. SLIGHT and R. SCOTT BURN, Engineers. Edited by HENRY STEPHENS. Large 8vo, uniform with 'The Book of the Farm,' £2, 2s.

STEVENSON. British Fungi. (Hymenomycetes.) By Rev. JOHN STEVENSON, Author of 'Mycologia Scotia,' Hon. Sec. Cryptogamic Society of Scotland. 2 vols. post 8vo, with Illustrations, price 12s. 6d. each. Vol. I. AGARICUS—BOLBITIUS. Vol. II. CORTINARIUS—DACRYMYCES.

STEWART. Advice to Purchasers of Horses. By JOHN STEWART, V.S., Author of 'Stable Economy.' New Edition. 2s. 6d.

—— Stable Economy. A Treatise on the Management of Horses in relation to Stabling, Grooming, Feeding, Watering, and Working. By JOHN STEWART, V.S. Seventh Edition, fcap. 8vo, 6s. 6d.

STORMONTH. Etymological and Pronouncing Dictionary of the English Language. Including a very Copious Selection of Scientific Terms. For Use in Schools and Colleges, and as a Book of General Reference. By the Rev. JAMES STORMONTH. The Pronunciation carefully Revised by the Rev. P. H. PHELP, M.A. Cantab. Ninth Edition, Revised throughout. Crown 8vo, pp. 800. 7s. 6d.

—— Dictionary of the English Language, Pronouncing, Etymological, and Explanatory. Revised by the Rev. P. H. PHELP. Library Edition. Imperial 8vo, handsomely bound in half morocco, 31s. 6d.

—— The School Etymological Dictionary and Word-Book. Combining the advantages of an ordinary pronouncing School Dictionary and an Etymological Spelling-book. Fourth Edition. Fcap. 8vo, pp. 254. 2s.

STORY. Nero; A Historical Play. By W. W. STORY, Author of 'Roba di Roma.' Fcap. 8vo, 6s.

—— Vallombrosa. Post 8vo, 5s.

—— He and She; or, A Poet's Portfolio. Fcap. 3s. 6d.

—— Poems. 2 vols. fcap., 7s. 6d.

—— Fiammetta. A Summer Idyl. Crown 8vo, 7s. 6d.

STRICKLAND. Life of Agnes Strickland. By her SISTER. Post 8vo, with Portrait engraved on Steel, 12s. 6d.

STURGIS. John-a-Dreams. A Tale. By JULIAN STURGIS. New Edition, crown 8vo, 3s. 6d.

—— Little Comedies, Old and New. Crown 8vo, 7s. 6d.

SUTHERLAND. Handbook of Hardy Herbaceous and Alpine Flowers, for general Garden Decoration. Containing Descriptions, in Plain Language, of upwards of 1000 Species of Ornamental Hardy Perennial and Alpine Plants, adapted to all classes of Flower-Gardens, Rockwork, and Waters; along with Concise and Plain Instructions for their Propagation and Culture. By WILLIAM SUTHERLAND, Landscape Gardener; formerly Manager of the Herbaceous Department at Kew. Crown 8vo, 7s. 6d.

TAYLOR. The Story of My Life. By the late Colonel MEADOWS TAYLOR, Author of 'The Confessions of a Thug,' &c. &c. Edited by his Daughter. New and cheaper Edition, being the Fourth. Crown 8vo, 6s.

THOLUCK. Hours of Christian Devotion. Translated from the German of A. Tholuck, D.D., Professor of Theology in the University of Halle. By the Rev. ROBERT MENZIES, D.D. With a Preface written for this Translation by the Author. Second Edition, crown 8vo, 7s. 6d.

THOMSON. Handy Book of the Flower-Garden: being Practical Directions for the Propagation, Culture, and Arrangement of Plants in Flower-Gardens all the year round. Embracing all classes of Gardens, from the largest to the smallest. With Engraved Plans, illustrative of the various systems of Grouping in Beds and Borders. By DAVID THOMSON, Gardener to his Grace the Duke of Buccleuch, K.T., at Drumlanrig. Fourth and Cheaper Edition, crown 8vo, 5s.

THOMSON. The Handy Book of Fruit-Culture under Glass : being a series of Elaborate Practical Treatises on the Cultivation and Forcing of Pines, Vines, Peaches, Figs, Melons, Strawberries, and Cucumbers. With Engravings of Hothouses, &c., most suitable for the Cultivation and Forcing of these Fruits. By DAVID THOMSON, Gardener to his Grace the Duke of Buccleuch, K.T., at Drumlanrig. Second Ed. Cr. 8vo, with Engravings, 7s. 6d.

THOMSON. A Practical Treatise on the Cultivation of the Grape-Vine. By WILLIAM THOMSON, Tweed Vineyards. Ninth Edition, 8vo, 5s.

THOMSON. Cookery for the Sick and Convalescent. With Directions for the Preparation of Poultices, Fomentations, &c. By BARBARA THOMSON. Fcap. 8vo, 1s. 6d.

THOTH. A Romance. Third Edition. Crown 8vo, 4s. 6d.

By the Same Author.

A DREAMER OF DREAMS. A Modern Romance. Crown 8vo, 6s.

TOM CRINGLE'S LOG. A New Edition, with Illustrations. Crown 8vo, cloth gilt, 5s. Cheap Edition, 2s.

TRANSACTIONS OF THE HIGHLAND AND AGRICUL-TURAL SOCIETY OF SCOTLAND. Published annually, price 5s.

TULLOCH. Rational Theology and Christian Philosophy in England in the Seventeenth Century. By JOHN TULLOCH, D.D., Principal of St Mary's College in the University of St Andrews; and one of her Majesty's Chaplains in Ordinary in Scotland. Second Edition. 2 vols. 8vo, 16s.

—— Modern Theories in Philosophy and Religion. 8vo, 15s.

—— Luther, and other Leaders of the Reformation. Third Edition, enlarged. Crown 8vo, 3s. 6d.

—— Memoir of Principal Tulloch, D.D., LL.D. By Mrs OLIPHANT, Author of 'Life of Edward Irving.' Third and Cheaper Edition. 8vo, with Portrait. 7s. 6d.

TWO STORIES OF THE SEEN AND THE UNSEEN. 'THE OPEN DOOR,' 'OLD LADY MARY.' Crown 8vo, cloth, 2s. 6d.

VEITCH. Institutes of Logic. By JOHN VEITCH, LL.D., Professor of Logic and Rhetoric in the University of Glasgow. Post 8vo, 12s. 6d.

—— The Feeling for Nature in Scottish Poetry. From the Earliest Times to the Present Day. 2 vols. fcap. 8vo, in roxburghe binding. 15s.

—— Merlin and Other Poems. Fcap. 8vo.

VIRGIL. The Æneid of Virgil. Translated in English Blank Verse by G. K. RICKARDS, M.A., and Lord RAVENSWORTH. 2 vols. fcap. 8vo, 10s.

WALFORD. The Novels of L. B. WALFORD. New and Uniform Edition. Crown 8vo, each 5s. *Sold separately.*
MR SMITH: A PART OF HIS LIFE.—COUSINS.—PAULINE.—TROUBLESOME DAUGHTERS.—DICK NETHERBY.—THE BABY'S GRANDMOTHER.—HISTORY OF A WEEK.

—— A Stiff-Necked Generation. 3 vols. post 8vo, 25s. 6d.

—— Four Biographies from 'Blackwood': Jane Taylor, Hannah More, Elizabeth Fry, Mary Somerville. Crown 8vo, 5s.

WARREN'S (SAMUEL) WORKS :—
Diary of a Late Physician. Cloth, 2s. 6d.; boards, 2s.
Ten Thousand A-Year. Cloth, 3s. 6d.; boards, 2s. 6d.
Now and Then. The Lily and the Bee. Intellectual and Moral Development of the Present Age. 4s. 6d.
Essays : Critical, Imaginative, and Juridical. 5s.

WARREN. The Five Books of the Psalms. With Marginal Notes. By Rev. SAMUEL L. WARREN, Rector of Esher, Surrey; late Fellow, Dean, and Divinity Lecturer, Wadham College, Oxford. Crown 8vo, 5s.

WATSON. Christ's Authority; and other Sermons. By the late ARCHIBALD WATSON, D.D., Minister of the Parish of Dundee, and one of Her Majesty's Chaplains for Scotland. With Introduction by the Very Rev. PRINCIPAL CAIRD, Glasgow. Crown 8vo, 7s. 6d.

WEBSTER. The Angler and the Loop-Rod. By DAVID WEBSTER.
Crown 8vo, with Illustrations, 7s. 6d.

WELLINGTON. Wellington Prize Essays on "the System of Field
Manœuvres best adapted for enabling our Troops to meet a Continental Army."
Edited by Lieut.-General Sir EDWARD BRUCE HAMLEY, K.C.B. 8vo, 12s. 6d.

WESTMINSTER ASSEMBLY. Minutes of the Westminster As-
sembly, while engaged in preparing their Directory for Church Government,
Confession of Faith, and Catechisms (November 1644 to March 1649). Edited
by the Rev. Professor ALEX. T. MITCHELL, of St Andrews, and the Rev. JOHN
STRUTHERS, LL.D. With a Historical and Critical Introduction by Professor
Mitchell. 8vo, 15s.

WHITE. The Eighteen Christian Centuries. By the Rev. JAMES
WHITE. Seventh Edition, post 8vo, with Index. 6s.

———— History of France, from the Earliest Times. Sixth Thousand, post 8vo, with Index, 6s.

WHITE. Archæological Sketches in Scotland—Kintyre and Knap- ✔
dale. By Colonel T. P. WHITE, R.E., of the Ordnance Survey. With numerous Illustrations. 2 vols. folio, £4, 4s. Vol. I., Kintyre, sold separately,
£2, 2s.

———— The Ordnance Survey of the United Kingdom. A Popular
Account. Crown 8vo, 5s.

WILLIAMSON. Poems of Nature and Life. By DAVID R.
WILLIAMSON, Minister of Kirkmaiden. Fcap. 8vo, 3s.

WILLS AND GREENE. Drawing-room Dramas for Children. By
W. G. WILLS and the Hon. Mrs GREENE. Crown 8vo, 6s.

WILSON. Works of Professor Wilson. Edited by his Son-in-Law,
Professor FERRIER. 12 vols. crown 8vo, £2, 8s.

———— Christopher in his Sporting-Jacket. 2 vols., 8s.

———— Isle of Palms, City of the Plague, and other Poems. 4s.

———— Lights and Shadows of Scottish Life, and other Tales. 4s.

———— Essays, Critical and Imaginative. 4 vols., 16s.

———— The Noctes Ambrosianæ. 4 vols., 16s.

———— Homer and his Translators, and the Greek Drama. Crown
8vo, 4s.

WINGATE. Annie Weir, and other Poems. By DAVID WINGATE.
Fcap. 8vo, 5s.

———— Lily Neil. A Poem. Crown 8vo, 4s. 6d.

WORDSWORTH. The Historical Plays of Shakspeare. With
Introductions and Notes. By CHARLES WORDSWORTH, D.C.L., Bishop of S
Andrews. 3 vols. post 8vo, each price 7s. 6d.

WORSLEY. Poems and Translations. By PHILIP STANHOPE
WORSLEY, M.A. Edited by EDWARD WORSLEY. Second Edition, enlarged.
Fcap. 8vo, 6s.

YATE. England and Russia Face to Face in Asia. A Record of
Travel with the Afghan Boundary Commission. By Captain A. C. YATE,
Bombay Staff Corps, Special Correspondent of the 'Pioneer,' 'Daily Telegraph,' &c., &c., with the Afghan Boundary Commission. 8vo, with Maps
and Illustrations, 21s.

YATE. Northern Afghanistan; or, Letters from the Afghan
Boundary Commission. By Major C. E. Yate, C.S.I., C.M.G. Bombay Staff
Corps, F.R.G.S. 8vo, with Maps. 18s.

YOUNG. A Story of Active Service in Foreign Lands. Compiled
from letters sent home from South Africa, India, and China, 1856-1882. By
Surgeon-General A. Graham Young, Author of 'Crimean Cracks.' Crown 8vo,
Illustrated, 7s. 6d.

YULE. Fortification: for the Use of Officers in the Army, and
Readers of Military History. By Col. YULE, Bengal Engineers. 8vo, with
numerous Illustrations, 10s. 6d.